Flying doesn't scare me. I've flown a lot, making personal appearance tours, filming on location, visiting my father when he's in New York, but this time I was nervous. Not because of the plane, but because of what was going to happen when the plane landed. My life was about to make one enormous change, and even though I wanted that change, had fantasized about it for years, it was a little disconcerting to have it be a reality. No career, a normal family, even a brand-new fully grown brother, all at once.

SUSAN BETH PFEFFER was graduated from New York University with a major in television, motion pictures, and radio. She is a native New Yorker and now lives in Middletown, New York. Her previous novels for teenagers include *Marly the Kid* and *The Beauty Queen*, both available in Laurel-Leaf editions.

Starring
Peter and
Leigh

Susan Beth Pfeffer

LAUREL-LEAF BOOKS bring together under a single imprint outstanding works of fiction and nonfiction particularly suitable for young adult readers, both in and out of the classroom. Charles F. Reasoner, Professor of Elementary Education, New York University, is consultant to this series.

Published by
Dell Publishing Co., Inc.
1 Dag Hammarskjold Plaza
New York, New York 10017

For Todd

ISBN: 0-440-98200-6

RL: 6.8

Reprinted by arrangement with Delacorte Press
Printed in the United States of America
First Laurel-Leaf printing—August 1980
Seventh Laurel-Leaf printing—April 1982

Starring
   Peter and
      Leigh

Chapter
1

Flying doesn't scare me. I've flown a lot, making personal appearance tours, filming on location, visiting my father when he's in New York, but this flight made me nervous. Not because of the plane, but because of what was going to happen when it landed. My life was about to make one enormous change, and even though I wanted that change, had fantasized about it for years, it was a little weird to know it would be a reality. No more career, a normal family, even a brand-new fully grown brother, all at once.

Retirement, I've heard, is frightening, no matter how many years you've had to prepare for it. I'd had about two months. That was when my mother married Ben Sanders. She'd known Ben for years; they had dated in high school, but Mom had dreams of being a star (or so Ben said) and ran off to New York, leaving Ben behind with a broken heart. They both eventually married other people, and each union produced one offspring (me, and Ben's son, Peter) and one divorce. So one day when Ben was in L.A. on business, he looked up Mom, and they rekindled the old flame. I was perfectly happy about it. Ben is a nice guy, and Mom was happier than she'd been in a long time. But Ben lived on Long Island and wasn't about to relocate, so Mom moved back there with him. I stayed on in L.A. for the summer since I was committed to doing a made-for-TV movie, but as soon as that was finished I waved good-bye to tinseltown and hopped the first plane east.

Mom's marriage did keep me from having to find new parts, now that my series had been canceled. I'd spent the past four years playing Chris Kampbell on *The Kampbell Kids*. I was the second oldest girl on the show, the one who had all the story lines about being too old to be cute and too young to be beautiful. That's what happens when you start a part at age twelve. It was not a conspicuous part. I was never the one swarmed around at state fairs. Mothers always favored Bobby

Phillips, who played Checkers, the youngest and cutest (he was the most obnoxious four-year-old I'd ever worked with, and by the time he was eight, he wasn't much better), and of course the girls always went for Barry Cooper, who played Chuck (or Up-Chuck, as we fondly called him off camera). Barry really hit it big with *The Kampbell Kids*. He was twenty-two when we started, but he looked like he was closer to sixteen, and even I had a crush on him for a while. (So did Natalie Collins and Joni McCarthy, who played my sisters. So did a few of our directors.) Oddly enough, Barry was a pretty nice guy. He treated us all gently when we swooned over him and seemed genuinely embarrassed when he was on the cover of *TV Guide* and *Time* magazine in the same week. We all knew he was thrilled, but he had the grace to make jokes about it.

We had a big party when we filmed our last show. I even kissed obnoxious little Bobby, who promptly pulled my braid and told me I was washed up, the little sweetheart. He won't know what washed up is until he starts looking around for parts for cute eight-year-old boys. Everyone knew I was leaving the business, so they were all extra specially nice to me. I got a lot of presents, including a charm bracelet with a charm of each of the regulars on it, and Barry gave me a kiss that was a little less brotherly than usual. We all vowed to keep in touch and cried a lot. (Even Joni and I hugged, and we hadn't spoken unless we had to for two years. It seemed a fitting conclusion to my Hollywood years. Except of course the next day I showed up for makeup and costume fittings and got back to work on the TV movie.

Right before I left, I'd turned down a couple of offers to perform in New York. None of them were very exciting, although there was a pimple commercial that was dying to have me. I didn't regret it. For four years I'd been playing Chris Kampbell, all-American kid, and believe me, it was pure guesswork. I had nothing to go on except what I'd seen on TV. I've never had the chance to be a normal kid. Instead, I've worked since I was six months old and starred along with my rear end in a diapers commercial. That was when Mom decided I might be a more marketable commodity than she was and retired to become a stage mother. I don't mean that as an insulting term. Granted, Mom wasn't a superstar, but she was making a living and could have kept going if she'd wanted. But I was a really cute infant and offers for me came in faster than offers for her, so she just resigned herself to managing my career. First I was in commercials and then three years on the soap opera *Tomorrow's Destiny*, playing somebody's illegitimate daughter, and then back to more commercials, a couple of plays (we were in New York then, the three of us), and a year on another soap, *Love Everlasting*, which only lasted a year. Then out to L.A. because I got a part in a Disney movie, and that led directly to *The Kampbell Kids*. Dad stayed behind, first for a part in a show and then for a divorce.

I've never been a star, but I've always worked steadily. That's what happens if you start young and stay blonde. Still, I could certainly understand why Mom gave it all up to marry Ben. I sure didn't mind giving it all up myself to move east and go to a regular high school and be a regular kid just like Chris Kampbell, only with fewer brothers and sisters. (Thank God. One stepbrother was enough to scare me.)

I knew Peter was seventeen, only one year older than I am, but I'd never met him because he never came out west with Ben. He has hemophilia and is often bedridden. How's that for cheery news? Peter hasn't always been stuck in bed. But for several months he has been, and they don't know when or even if he'll get well enough to lead a fairly normal life. Hemophiliacs never lead completely normal lives, Ben told me. Ben told me a lot about Peter because Peter lives with him. I never asked where Peter's mother was, but she wasn't there taking care of Peter. That was left to Ben, who obviously adored his son. Ben talked about other things; it wasn't always Peter this or Peter that, but Peter seemed to be behind everything Ben said. Ben called him every night and spoke with him for at least half an hour, which is an expensive habit. Peter was very smart. He'd read every book in the public library at least twice, so Ben had taken out a New York City library card and Peter sent him in once a week to take out more books. Peter wrote poetry. Peter played chess. Peter handled his misfortunes with the patience of a saint. And so on. No wonder I was terrified to meet him.

Besides, how was he going to react to me? It had just been him and his father and a housekeeper for years. Now suddenly he had a stepmother who knew nothing about sons although a great deal about negotiating contracts, and a stepsister who knew nothing about brothers except what she'd learned pretending to have them. Poor Peter. I was sure he was going to hate me, and I didn't blame him.

Which is why I was a little more nervous than usual when the plane landed.

Ben and Mom met me at the airport. They were waiting at the gate for me and we exchanged hugs.

I embraced Mom a little longer than usual because it had been so long since I'd seen her and I needed reassurance, and then we went to the luggage area and got my suitcases. I'd shipped most of my stuff earlier, but I'd taken a couple of suitcases' worth to tide me over until my trunks came. I wore my charm bracelet.

Ben piled Mom, the bags, and me into his station wagon and drove us home. It had been a long time since I'd seen Long Island, so I looked at the scenery while I answered questions about the flight and the weather and how the TV movie had gone. It had gone rather well, I thought. The role was much harder than I'd been used to and I'd enjoyed the challenge. Besides, it was a nice swan song.

"Peter's eager to meet you," Ben said. "He's been watching *The Kampbell Kids* all summer. Actually, he always watches it, but this summer he's been concentrating his attentions on you."

"Peter watches a lot of TV," Mom said.

"Thank God for it," Ben said. "It gives him something to occupy his mind. Especially in the summer when there's no tutoring."

"Peter doesn't go to school?" I said, to make sure.

"He's had a tutor for the past few months," Ben said. "We talked about having the tutor come in for the summer, just to give Peter something to do, but as it is, Peter's far ahead of his class academically, so we couldn't see any advantage to it."

"Peter's very smart," Mom said.

If he was so smart, I couldn't see why he was watching *The Kampbell Kids*, which requires a mental age of two years to enjoy, but it was nice to know Peter was doing research on me. At least he wasn't ignoring the problem.

"It's been rough on him having his leg in a cast all summer," Ben said.

"It's amazing how patient Peter is. He never complains," Mom said.

"I only wish he would," Ben said. "It would make things easier if he did."

Saint Peter all right. I complain constantly.

"Well, this is it," Ben said and pulled the car into a driveway. There was a nice-sized expanse of land and a ranch house. I was a little disappointed. There were plenty of ranch houses in California; I'd been hoping for something more colonial.

Ben took my bags and Mom opened the front door. She seemed a little nervous about it and had trouble getting the door unlocked, but on the second try she managed and we all went in. It was pleasantly cool inside and there were certain touches in the living room I could identify as Mom's: a lot of plants, a framed picture of me.

Mom gave me a quick tour of the house while Ben checked in on Peter. I'd been given a nice room, pretty and feminine. It looked a lot like Chris Kampbell's room. Mom's idea of normal kids was based on TV too.

"How's it going, Mom?" I asked as I put my suitcase down.

"Pretty well," Mom said. "Better than I thought it would, frankly. Peter's very nice and he's made a real effort to get along. I think you'll like him."

"Do you miss L.A.?"

"Not particularly," Mom said. "Don't forget, this is where I came from. So I've just come back home."

There was a knock on the door and Ben came in. "Peter's asking to meet you," he said. "Do you think you're ready for introductions?"

"Of course," I said. There are some advantages to being a professional actress. It makes lying a lot easier. So Mom and I followed Ben through a hallway and a room or two and another hallway until we reached what was obviously an occupied room. It was easy to tell since the stereo was blaring.

"Peter," Ben said as we came in. "I don't suppose we could lower that thing."

"Sure, Dad," Peter said and grinned. He had a nice grin. I'd seen pictures of him, but they didn't show what a nice smile he had. Peter had long brown hair, gold-rimmed glasses, and a slightly owlish look.

"Peter, this is my daughter," Mom said. "Leigh, this is Peter."

"Hi," I said quietly.

"Hi," he said a good deal more cheerfully. "You look better in real life."

"Oh hell," I said. I hate it when people say things like that. It always makes me feel slightly unreal.

Peter laughed. "I'm sorry," he said. "I like your haircut."

"Thank you," I said, wondering if I should apologize for saying hell. "Cutting off that braid was the first thing I did when the show was over."

"Well," Ben said and cleared his throat. "Maybe we should give the young people a chance to talk. Shall we go, Angie?"

"That's a good idea," Mom said in her officious voice. She and Ben left the room. Peter and I stared at each other.

"I like your mother," Peter said. "You want to sit down?"

"Thank you," I said and sat in a chair where I could face him. He didn't look nearly as terrifying as I thought he would. I'd pictured him surrounded by nurses and life support systems, but there was just him and the bed, which I could hardly see for all the junk on it. "I like Ben a lot."

"They seem to be happy," Peter said. "And Angie's been trying hard with me. I appreciate it."

"She said you've been making an effort with her," I said. "She appreciates it too."

"I'm not hard to get along with," he said. "Does that surprise you?"

"A little," I said, but I was pleased to hear it.

"There's this concept about invalids," he said. "That they're difficult and demanding. Which isn't to say I can't be. I can be hell at times. I may not even mean to be, but it just comes out that way."

"I stand warned," I said.

"Are you temperamental?" he asked.

"No," I said. "Temperamental kid actresses tend not to work steady."

Peter grinned again. "It's the whole thing about adjusting," he said. "We've both had to adjust to what we are more than other people, I think. I've been in and out of schools, in and out of friendships. Even my parents' divorce."

"I know what you mean," I said. "But this is my last adjustment. I'm retired now. Just like Garbo."

"Retired," he said. "You've really quit the business?"

"Forever and always," I said. "I've hung my acting shoes up."

"Do you mind?" he asked.

"Not yet," I said. "And I don't think I ever will. It was okay. I don't mind having done it, and it's nice to know I have all that money saved up, but frankly I want something else."

"What do you want?" he asked, staring at me.

"What everyone else has," I said. "Saturday night dates. Football games. Real classes. I guess that sounds dumb to you."

"Not at all," he said. "It sounds great."

"I've never had that kind of life," I said. "I've playacted it, but that's as close as I've gotten. The past four years I haven't even gone to school. I've been taught on the set with the other kids."

"I miss school," Peter said. "I never played football though."

"I should hope not," I said.

Peter laughed and then flinched suddenly.

"Are you okay?" I asked, afraid he was going to die right in front of me.

"I'm okay," he said. "The pain comes and goes."

"Should I call Ben?"

"No, you don't have to," he said. "He knows the pain comes and goes."

"It must be horrible," I said.

"It isn't fun," he said and swallowed hard. "It's

okay, really. I feel a lot better already. Just don't pay attention when I look funny."

"Don't look so funny then," I said.

Peter laughed. "I'm really glad you've moved here," he said. "I get so lonely."

"I can imagine," I said.

"Not that I expect you to spend all your time here keeping me company," he said. "You're not my nursemaid. Besides, I'm so used to being alone, I wouldn't like having someone hanging around me all the time. It would make me nervous."

"Okay," I said. "But I don't know much about hemophilia. Ben told me a little bit, but frankly I wasn't listening all that hard."

Peter laughed. "There are more interesting topics."

"How does it work?" I asked. "If you cut yourself, you can't stop bleeding?"

"Cuts aren't a problem," he said. "A bandage usually takes care of them. The problem is internal bleeding."

"But that's serious," I said.

"You got it," he said. "You want your explanation quick and superficial or slow and detailed?"

"Quick and superficial," I said.

"Okay," he said. "Bumping into things, which I do all the time, can cause bleeding. So can tension. Or sometimes it just starts for no good reason. If

13

I think I'm going to bleed, I take some stuff that helps ward it off. But most of the time I can't predict, and then I bleed and my father gives me transfusions. We keep the clotting factor I need in the house just in case."

"And you're never going to get any better?" I asked.

"Yes and no," he said. "I'll never be a professional wrestler. But the teen-age years are the worst because the body is still growing. And I'm a late bloomer. I keep getting taller. That puts strain on my joints, which is where I bleed the most: knees, elbows."

"But you won't be bedridden forever?"

"No," he said. "This is temporary. But there's been permanent damage to my knees, and I have arthritis, which doesn't help matters. Still, it could be worse."

"How?" I asked.

"At least I have my looks," he said grinning. "It's just a question of finding the right girl to be bed-ridden with."

"I would have been better off paying more attention to Ben," I said.

"At least you could come in sometimes and just talk," he said. "Tell me how things are in the real world. I feel so divorced from it sometimes."

"Don't you have friends?" I asked.

"Not many," he said. "People tend to be scared of me."

"I won't be," I said, feeling less scared already. "And of course I'll come in and talk. If I talk too much just kick me out."

"It's a deal," he said. "You must be really tired."

"I'm feeling a little hyper," I admitted.

"I suppose you'd like to go to your room and go to sleep," he said.

"Not particularly," I said. "I'd rather wind down first."

"Would you mind talking with me?" he asked. "I really want to hear what it was like on *The Kampbell Kids*. I watch it all the time."

"Why?" I asked.

"I watch everything," he said. "And I like shows about people my own age."

"I'd love to tell you about *The Kampbell Kids*. Here," I said and took off my charm bracelet to show him. "This is what they gave me at the farewell party. . . ."

Chapter
2

"We can do it," Peter said to me a couple of days later.

"Do what?" I asked. I was sitting in the easy chair next to his bed and feeling remarkably comfortable. I'm really not a shy person and there didn't seem to be any point being shy with Peter anyway, not if we were going to be sharing home and parents.

"Make you a normal person," he said.

"Thanks," I said. "I wasn't aware my horns showed."

"You know what I mean," he said. "I've been giving it a lot of thought and I think we can carry it off."

"You're going to have to make yourself a little clearer," I said. "I don't have the slightest idea what you're talking about."

"That's what you want, right?" he said. "To be accepted as just one of the kids? To lead a Chris Kampbell kind of life?"

"You know it is," I said.

"It isn't going to be easy," he said. "But if we work on it together I think we can do it."

"I don't understand what the problem is," I said. "I'm going to go to high school and do normal things and be a normal kid. What trick is there to that?"

"Because, Leigh, you aren't a normal kid. You're Leigh Thorpe, semistar. And all the other kids are going to treat you that way, at least for a while, and you're going to act that way too, especially if they're reinforcing it with their behavior." Peter looked very proud of himself.

"Good grief," I said. "Are you saying that I'm not going to be normal unless I follow some strange set of rules?"

"That's exactly what I'm telling you," he said.

"I don't suppose there's a handbook?"

"I didn't have time to write one," Peter said. "Look, I went to school, I have some vague recollection of what it was like. Clothes. Have you given any thought to clothes?"

"I planned to wear some," I said.

"But what kind?" he persisted. "The wrong outfit could set you back for months. But I could tell you what to wear, what the other kids are wearing. Things like that. The two of us together could manage one normal person."

I thought about it. I could see Peter had a point. What did I really know about being normal? There was a chance, not a small one either, that life wasn't anything like *The Kampbell Kids*. And I could blow the real thing with one or two false moves. It was like an audition. I would only get the part if I gave a good first reading. And I didn't have any preparation for the part.

"What's in it for you?" I asked Peter. Years in show business taught me always to look a gift horse in the mouth.

"What do you mean?" he asked.

"Why should you help me out?" I asked.

"You see you do need help?"

"Yeah," I said. "But why are you so willing to help me?"

"Because it would be fun," he said.

I stared at him.

"I've spent most of my life in this house," he said. "The rest has been pretty evenly divided between schools and hospitals. And I've missed out on a lot of things as a result. Normal things. Things we've talked about."

I nodded.

"With you around I have a chance to enjoy some of what I've missed. Granted, it'll be a vicarious experience, but believe me, I'm an expert in the vicarious. I know how to milk it for every pleasurable moment. Now you can go to school and maybe get accepted in a few months and tell me dribs and drabs of it and I'd be satisfied. But if we go at it together, figure out the shortcuts, make the decisions together, you'd have the benefit of my expertise and I'd have the chance to actually do something. I never get to do things. That's what's in it for me."

He looked at me with those appealing eyes of his. Turning him down would have felt like kicking an orphan.

"Okay," I said. "You're right about all this being a lot more complicated than I thought it would be. And if I have an expert around, I might as well use him."

Peter smiled.

"Although I do want to know how you acquired so much expertise if you were hardly at school," I said.

"Because when I was there I watched," he said. "I didn't have many friends. It's hard to sustain a friendship if you're always going off to the hospital or staying in bed. And I couldn't do most of those normal boy things, which cut down on my friends too. So I watched. If I couldn't actually participate, I'd observe. I'm a fantastic observer."

"Do I get my money back if you make mistakes?" I asked.

"I won't make any," he said. "I want you to be a success as much as you do. And like I said, I've been giving all this a lot of thought. You don't have to worry."

I knew I'd worry like crazy anyway, but there was no point saying so. "All right, Svengali," I said. "What's the first step in being normal?"

"You have to look average," he said. "As average as you can look. Take your hair."

"Is it too messy?" I asked. "I was thinking about getting it trimmed before school started."

"That's exactly what I mean," he said. "If you look too neat it'll take away from your averageness."

"But the other girls'll be getting haircuts for school," I said.

"They can afford to," he said. "They want to look their best. You don't."

I could understand his logic, just as I could understand his adamant refusal to let me try out for cheerleaders, much as I argued.

"But why not?" I said when the subject came up. "There's nothing more American than being a cheerleader."

"Because you'll look like a show-off if you do," he said.

"But I know how to do those cheers and everything," I said.

"Exactly," he said. "And how did you learn those cheers?"

"The choreographer taught me," I said.

"Great," he said. "You think the other girls have choreographers to help them out?"

"But Chris was a cheerleader," I said. "I bet the kids'll be surprised if I don't try out. Besides, maybe I'll look like a snob if I don't."

"You'll look more like one if you do," he said. "Maybe next year, when you're more accepted. Right now you have to keep a low profile."

"A low shaggy one," I grumbled, but I could see what he meant. I was resigned to being conspicuous, at least in the beginning. I figured my novelty would wear off as the year went on. True,

The Kampbell Kids was scheduled for nightly re-runs at six P.M., but they'd probably be starting the series at the beginning when I was twelve and looked it. By the time they hit me at sixteen I'd be a regular class member, or so I hoped.

Mom, who sensed my nervousness without totally understanding it, assured me she'd consulted with the principal when she'd enrolled me at Madison High and he'd told her I'd be treated just the same as everyone else. Peter, however, was skeptical about that.

"Sure he said it," Peter said. "What was he supposed to say? That you'd be called on to deliver a testimonial to the teaching staff of Madison High?"

"How is the teaching staff?" I asked.

"Adequate," he said. "Some good teachers, some lousy ones. Same as anywhere. But that's not the point."

"No, I suppose not," I said.

"The point is you are different, and you're going to be treated differently. There's going to be at least one teacher and several kids who'll be gunning for you, and you're better off if you're expecting it."

"Oh, come on now," I said. "It's not like I'm Shirley Temple."

"You're famous enough," he said. "What you've

got to do is get as many kids on your side as possible, so if anything does happen you'll have their support."

"You make it sound like I'm going to be lynched."

Peter ignored me. "You have to be gracious," he said. "That's the whole key. Gracious without being condescending."

"Gracious?" I said. "I've never been gracious in my life. I'm not royalty, you know."

"Friendly then," he said. "But not overeager. But smiling a lot, saying hi to everybody. Gracious."

"Gracious," I said with a sigh. "I can't wait until I run for president and you run my PR campaign."

"No school offices," he said. "Not this year."

"I meant president of the United States," I said. "Don't you have any ambitions?"

"I have my share," he said. "Now go out there and be normal."

So for the first day of school I put on a nice pair of slacks and an equally nice blouse (a dress was too dressy, a skirt too deliberately high schoolish, and jeans too sloppy in Peter's opinion), carried my nice neat brand-new loose-leaf notebook (I had one from the year before that Peter vetoed because of its University of Southern California decal. I'd just always assumed I'd go there), and walked to school. I'd walked there twice the day before, to get the feeling of it and prevent myself from getting lost when the dress rehearsals ended and the show went on. Because for all of Peter's and my discussions about normalcy, it was all just an act as far as I was concerned. Probably as far as he was concerned too; he just wasn't admitting it to me.

When I got there there were hundreds of kids pressing around the front door of the school trying to find out what their homeroom assignments were and I pressed in with them, forgetting graciousness immediately. It didn't matter. Nobody knew who I was, although a few kids did seem to do double takes when I said excuse me to them.

I was in Mr. Taylor's homeroom, room 208, and I found it without too much difficulty. I took a seat and waited. In the meantime I stared at the kids and was stared at in return. It didn't make me nervous, since it was only logical they'd look at the new kid. I smiled as graciously as I could manage and checked out people's outfits. I seemed to have dressed properly, which was a relief. I began to think Peter's judgment was trustworthy.

Mr. Taylor called out the roll and assigned us our seats alphabetically. As soon as he called out my full name, four kids went, "Oh." That was all it was going to take, I knew. I smiled some more.

The principal talked on the loudspeaker and wished us all a happy and productive school year, but the class didn't pay any attention to him since they were all whispering about me. Eventually he went off the air and Mr. Taylor said he had an announcement to make.

"We have, as some of you may have realized, something of a celebrity in our homeroom this year," he said. "Leigh Thorpe is a TV star of some reknown. Leigh, would you care to stand up?"

I cared to stand on his toes, but I stood up and smiled instead.

"What Miss Thorpe of course does not know is that once again I will be directing the junior class play," Mr. Taylor said. "Perhaps we'll be fortunate enough to have her star in our little show."

Just what I needed. A director. I smiled some more, ready to kill, and sat down. I thought about looking down, pretending to check out my schedule, but decided that would be an admission of defeat and kept on staring straight ahead.

The buzzer rang and I joined the rest of the kids as we went to our different classes. I knew I couldn't be the only topic of conversation in the hallway, but it didn't help my paranoia. I wondered if I should just give up on being normal and be my regular self for the year. Then I thought about Peter and started smiling again.

The morning actually went all right, except for five different kids who bumped into me (which was easy enough to do, since I didn't have the slightest idea where I was going) and said, "Excuse me, Chris." Fool that I was, I answered to it, at first because I felt more at home in a school if I pretended I was Chris, and then because it was easier than saying, "The name's Leigh, dammit, and don't forget it." Also more gracious. The classes weren't too bad, although there was a reaction every time one of the teachers called my name. At least none of them made any little speeches about my star status.

I dreaded lunch, and as I sat down in the cafeteria I knew I was right to. I got looked at a lot and nobody sat down anywhere near me. I could understand that they might think I was unapproachable (if nothing else I was on a first-name basis with Barry Cooper), but I didn't know what I could do to let them know all I wanted was to be one of the gang.

My isolation ended when a tall dark-haired girl sat down across from me. "Do you mind if I join you?" she asked.

"Not at all," I said, smiling genuinely.

"Please forgive my curiosity," she said, "but we're in the same French class, and gym too, I think, and I've noticed everyone's been buzzing about you. I was wondering why."

"Oh," I said. "Didn't anyone tell you?"

"I don't have many friends in this school," she said. I could imagine why easily enough. She was wearing a stylish dress, and even though she was wearing only a trace of makeup, she looked considerably more sophisticated than anyone else I'd seen. One of the looks Peter had vetoed for me.

"My name is Leigh Thorpe," I said. "I'm an actress."

"How delightful," she said. "My name is Anna Lessing. Have I seen you in anything?"

"I was Chris on *The Kampbell Kids* for the past four years," I said.

"Excuse me?" she said. "Was that on Broadway?"

"No, it was a TV show," I said.

"Oh, that explains it," she said. "Our TV has been broken for a few years."

"Really," I said, delighted to meet someone even more freakish than me.

"We've been meaning to get it fixed," Anna said. "We've just never gotten around to it. I do go to the theater a lot. Have you done any theater?"

"Not in years," I said.

"Then I probably wouldn't remember you even

if I had seen you," she said. "Are you here for any reason?"

"To go to school," I said, feeling foolish. One of the advantages of being a pro is that you feel much older than kids your own age, but Anna made me feel like a baby. She had a way of looking directly at you that was very disconcerting.

"I mean on the East Coast," she said. "At this dreary school."

"I've retired," I said. "My mother married a man who lives here and I'm living with her."

"I see," she said thoughtfully. "It must be a difficult adjustment."

"Right now it is," I said. "Everyone's been staring at me."

"Yes, I've noticed," she said. "You must understand, the kids here don't have that much excitement in their lives. You're quite an event for them."

I tittered nervously.

"I could tell you were different," she said. "There was an air about you, a worldly quality."

My old producer would have dropped dead if he'd heard me described as worldly. I felt vaguely flattered.

"Have you done much film work?" she asked.

"Just a Disney movie," I said, afraid I was joining the Philistines.

"Oh," she said. "I suppose there aren't that many good parts for teen-agers."

"I just did a made-for-TV movie I'm very proud of," I said. "It was a really challenging part, much different from what I'd been doing."

"Maybe my parents will get the set fixed by the time it's on," Anna said. "Do you think you'll resume your acting career?"

"I don't plan to," I said.

"Do you want to direct?" she asked.

"No," I said.

"I've thought about directing," she said. "Film would be my first choice."

I tried to think about something to say about film directing. "Difficult work," I said.

"Please forgive me for rambling," Anna said. "It's simply that I feel so isolated in this environment. It's so rare to meet someone here with even the vaguest aura of intelligence."

I preferred worldliness, but I was willing to take any compliment. "Do you feel left out?" I asked.

"Certainly not," she said. "High school activities don't interest me at all. Football. Petty rivalries. Proms. It's all so childish."

"I think it might be fun," I said.

"You'll get tired of it soon enough," Anna said. "I live for the day I can get out of here. As a matter of fact, I think I'll skip my senior year altogether and go straight on to college."

"Do you know where you want to go?" I asked.

"Anywhere," she said. "Just as long as it isn't on Long Island."

I grinned. Her hatred had a refreshing quality to it.

Anna stared at me and then laughed. "You're looking at a desperate woman," she said. "Trapped in the body of a sixteen-year-old girl. I know I sound funny, but I can't help it. That's just the way I am. But I hope we become friends. I'd appreciate a friendship with someone like you. Someone who knows there's more to life than football games."

"I'd like it too," I said. Having a crazy friend seemed a lot easier than trying to pass for normal.

The bell rang and we got up and walked to the door. "I'll see you later if we have any more classes together," Anna said. "Otherwise I'll see you tomorrow in French."

I smiled good-bye and we started to wend our way through the hallways. When Anna and I found ourselves in the same chemistry class we took seats next to each other. I was glad to have some protection against the whispers.

I thought Peter would be happy for me. After

all, a friend on the first day of school is nothing to sneeze at. But he got hysterical instead.

"Not Anna Lessing," he said. "She's crazy."

"How would you know?" I said angrily.

"I was there when she first started school," he said. "I didn't leave until November, and by then everybody knew about Anna Lessing."

"I liked her," I said.

"Sometimes I wonder about you," he said. "You actually like that snot?"

"I know she's a snot," I said. "She's affected as hell. But she had the nerve to come up to me and start a conversation. She didn't just stare."

"You said she didn't know who you were," Peter said. "Besides, you knew it would take the other kids a while to start approaching you."

"They all hate me," I said flatly.

"They do not," Peter said. "But they all hate Anna, and if you start hanging out with her, they'll figure you're as crazy as she is."

"Maybe I am," I said. "Maybe I'll never fit in. What do I have in common with those kids anyway?"

"Not much," Peter said. "Not right now. But I thought what you wanted was to become like them."

"Yeah," I said.

"Is that what Anna wants?"

"She wants to get out as fast as she can," I said.

"If you want to hang out with the class rebels, that's fine, do it," Peter said. "I don't know who they are in your class, but I'm sure there's a group of them. There are a lot of reasonable groups. You don't have to hang out with the football players. But if you make friends with a dyed-in-the-wool weirdo like Anna Lessing, it'll just be you and her for the rest of the year. Is that what you want?"

"No," I said. A full year of Anna could get to be very tiring.

Peter looked calmer. "Did you smile a lot?" he asked.

"Every goddamn minute," I said.

He smiled. "Were you gracious?" he asked.

"The Queen could take lessons from me," I said.

"Okay," he said. "I know you want it all to happen right away, but it's going to take time. So just relax but watch out who you're seen with. One more Anna Lessing and you're done for."

I thought about asking Peter if he'd been the Anna Lessing in his class but thought better of it. Besides, I didn't want to hear if he had been and I was afraid that was what he'd say. So I excused myself and went to the living room to give my mother a censored account of my first day at school.

Peter of course didn't give me detailed instructions on how to deal with Anna. Some things had to be left to my own discretion. So I decided to be honest. The truth, I've found, when properly presented, can be as effective as a lie.

I waited until lunch, since there seemed no other convenient time to do it. We met at the cafeteria and took two seats by ourselves. Anna immediately began chattering; I waited until she finished before I began my pitch.

"I've been giving a lot of thought to the things we said yesterday," I said, which certainly was true. "And I'm afraid I might have misrepresented myself."

"How do you mean?" Anna asked, biting into her tuna fish sandwich. "You really aren't a star?"

"No, of course not," I said. "I mean, I am an actress, was, but not a star. I didn't say I was a star, did I?"

"I got that impression from somewhere," she said. "Perhaps from all the buzzing. Everyone is buzzing, you know."

"I know," I said. "But that's not what I mean. About my acting. That isn't how I misrepresented myself."

"How then?" she asked. "I don't think we talked about anything else."

"We did," I said. "We talked about the other kids."

"Ah, them," she said. "I'd forgotten all about them."

"But you see, I don't want to," I said.

Anna stared at me. "I don't know what you mean," she said.

"I mean, that is to say, well, frankly, I want to assimilate," I said. It had taken me twenty sleepless minutes the night before to settle on that word.

"You can't mean you want to be like them," she said, gesturing at "them" with her tuna sandwich.

"That's just what I mean," I said, starting to feel desperate.

"For heaven's sake, why?" she asked.

"Because I've never been like them. I want to give it a chance."

"I've never been like them either, thank goodness," Anna said. "I've never been like a leper either, but I'm not about to join a colony just for the experience."

Again I was tempted to give it all up and be different like Anna, but I remembered Peter's grim resolution and tried again. "You chose not to be like them," I said. "That's fine, that's free will. But I've never had the chance. I may hate it, but I want to find out."

"You'll be bored silly," she said.

"Maybe," I said. "Or maybe I'll like it. I don't know."

Anna looked at me. "Let me guess where this conversation is leading," she said. "You don't think it would be that good an idea if we became friends."

"No," I said. "I'd love us to be friends. I like you."

"But . . ."

"But I don't just want to sit around and put everybody else down," I said. "I refuse to do that. This may be the only chance I'll ever have to be average, and I'm not about to blow it."

Anna laughed.

"I'm sorry," I said.

"No, it's all right," she said. "I'm used to being unpopular."

"Don't be a martyr about it," I said. "I want to be your friend. I just want to be other people's friend too."

"Shall we meet on the sly?" she asked. "Midnight rendezvous where none of the really popular kids will see us?"

"Name the place," I said.

"I'm not offended," she said. "I ought to be, but I'm not. I think it's your hair. It's impossible to take blondes seriously."

I smiled wanly.

"Very well," she said. "I don't want to keep you from becoming prom queen. Let me know how you like it."

"Anna," I said, but it was too late. She got up and took her lunch tray with her to a deserted corner of the cafeteria. And I was left alone to ponder what I was doing and why and whether it was too late to call the whole thing off and go back to California. But I knew there was no going back. So I ate my lunch and tried to think gracious thoughts.

Chapter
3

Peter and I had analyzed at length just what I should wear to school, but we hadn't taken into account underwear. It simply hadn't occurred to me, and frankly even if it had, I don't think I would have cared to discuss it with Peter.

So when we changed into our gym suits for the first time I found myself in the world of real underwear. It was quite a revelation.

Anna, for one, wore only a pair of bikini underpants. Most of the other girls were in bras and panties, neat but not flashy. And then there was me.

I wear real high-class underwear. My bras always had to be the best, because *The Kampbell Kids* producers were always very nervous about things like that, and my mother firmly believed there was no point wearing a really good bra if you didn't have really good underpants to match. I like satins and silks, in soft, sexy colors, and lace and embroidery. My underwear tended to be of the hand-launder-or-else variety.

Which would have been okay except that the first time I changed in that locker room everybody was looking at me. Most of the girls tried to sneak their looks, so it wouldn't be obvious that they were checking me out, but they all did. Some just plain stared as I took my clothes off. I realized they were curious about what my body looked like, and I wouldn't have minded that too much, since my body was just fine. One extra pound meant public humiliation on the set, and I hadn't gained any weight since coming east. Besides, I'd known I'd be checked out that first day, which was why I'd put on my very best underwear for the occasion.

Except it was much too good. The other girls looked positively ratty in comparison.

There didn't seem to be much I could do except change quickly, which I did. The girls were whispering among themselves anyway. I felt very lonely until Anna came over to me.

"Nice duds," she said. "You ought to wear them on the outside of your clothes and give everyone something really big to talk about."

I stared at her for a moment and then started giggling. "How was I supposed to know about underwear?"

"Now you know," she said. "Are you going to go out and buy something in basic cotton?"

"I think I'd better," I said as we started walking out of the locker room into the gym. "Have lunch with me?"

"No, I don't think so," she said.

"Why not?" I asked.

"Because I'd be an impediment to your progress," she said. "When you don't care about underwear anymore, then we'll have lunch together."

"You're making things more difficult than they have to be," I said.

"Funny," she said. "I was thinking the same thing about you."

So I had another lonely lunch, which I spent alternately cursing Peter and thinking about how I could convince Mom to accompany me and her charge card on a shopping spree to buy boring underwear.

For the most part, though, I really liked school those first few days. I couldn't get over how much things looked like school on *The Kampbell Kids*. Granted, we'd shot locations at a real school, but the students we'd used had all been professional extras and the teachers had all been actors and I'd never believed any of it.

But this was a real American high school, and it looked like a real American high school. I was delighted. I loved the classes too. Even when I'd lived in New York, I'd gone to professional children's schools, where kids were constantly coming in and out from auditions or performances and it was no trick at all to be absent. But here you started the day with everybody and you finished the day with the same everybody. And in the actual classes we all sat there and took notes on the exact same things and did the same homework. And we participated. We had class discussions. At *The Kampbell Kids* set we had a little room we used for school, but since our schedule was so tight and we were all different ages with different class levels, we never got a chance to talk with each other. Which, considering the tension there, probably wasn't a bad idea. The only thing we ever did talk about was how much we envied Barry Cooper and Natalie Collins, who were too old for school.

Here, though, we were all in it together. And kids chattered all the time, in the hallways and the girls' room, and in the locker room and before classes began. During lunch, which I persisted in eating in the cafeteria, everybody chattered to their hearts' content while I sat there and ate my all-American sandwiches all alone by my all-American self. After I'd rebuffed Anna and then been rebuffed by her in return, I could hardly ask if I could join her. So I ate alone. Tuna salad tastes awful if you eat it alone.

The first few days I blamed Peter and his lousy advice about Anna, but by the second week I decided to be mature about it and blame myself. Nobody forced me to do what he'd said. I had just about decided I was a rotten person and destined for a life of loneliness when a girl with bright red hair and a cheerful smile walked up to me at my little section of cafeteria.

"I'm Cathy Parker," she said. "We're in English together, and math."

"Oh, yeah," I said. "Hi."

"Everybody in this school's been talking about you and it just occurred to me and my friends that nobody's talking to you," she said. "So I got elected."

I smiled, nongraciously. "I have been feeling a little lonely," I admitted.

"We're just all terrified," she said. "That's why I'm here. I have more guts than anybody else."

"I'm not that scary," I said. "At least I never thought I was."

"You're a celebrity," she said. "And we're just not used to being around celebrities."

"I'm really not that famous," I said.

"You are to us," Cathy said. "I've watched you every week on *The Kampbell Kids* for years now. You were always the one I identified with because you were the one who was my age."

I smiled. At state fairs that was when they asked for my autograph. If Cathy had, I would have burst into tears.

"You cut your hair," she said instead.

"I got sick of that stupid braid," I said. "Besides, they wanted my hair in a different style for a TV movie I just did. So I had it all cut off."

"It looks great," she said. "It makes you look older."

"Thank you," I said. "That braid was a real drag."

"What are you doing here?" she asked. "Have you moved here?"

"Uh huh," I said. "My mother married a man who lives here."

"So you're not acting anymore?"

"I'm retired," I said.

"Why did you give it up?" she asked. "I never would if I had a chance like that."

"Because I want to be like you," I said. "I've always worked. I want to have some fun."

"You think this is fun?" Cathy said. "Wait until midterms."

"I didn't think it would all be fun," I said. "But I wanted to give it a try."

"I can understand that," she said. "You're nothing like I thought you'd be."

"What did you think I'd be like?" I asked.

"Like a movie star," she said. "Sunglasses all the time. You know."

"I know," I said. "I've worked with people like that."

"You have?" she asked. "I want to hear everything."

I wondered how that fit into the grand scheme of things and decided it was a reasonable way into the inner circles. "It's not that interesting," I said, "but I'll answer anything you want to ask."

"What I really want to know is if you ever went out with Barry Cooper," she said. "I had a crush on him for years."

I laughed. That was usually the question I got asked after the autograph. "I never dated him," I said. "He's ten years older than I am. But he kissed me real good at our farewell party."

"He did?" Cathy said. "What was it like?"

"Fantastic," I said.

"You actually kissed Barry Cooper," she said. "Wait until I tell everybody. No, wait, come back with me and you can tell us all. I want to hear every detail."

"There aren't that many details," I said, but Cathy had already grabbed my arm and started taking me back to her table. I took my books and went with her.

"Everybody, this is Leigh," Cathy said. "Leigh, this is Bob and Sharon and Andy. Leigh kissed Barry Cooper. Really kissed him."

I turned bright red. One of the others scolded Cathy, who apologized. Soon I was sitting with them telling them all about my days as a Kampbell Kid.

I spent the rest of the school day being introduced to people. The barrier had been broken and I was being fussed over by everybody, it seemed. I smiled all the time, tried to remember names (not always that easy with so many different faces surrounding me), and recounted to at least twenty people what it felt like to be kissed by Barry Cooper. I thought about sending him a note letting him know just how popular he was.

I kept an eye out for Anna, since the more I talked with other people, the worse I felt about her, but she was keeping to herself. I did notice her watching me a couple of times, but when I tried to draw her into the conversation she withdrew. I couldn't blame her, since I was the one who had dumped her. Still, I would have liked to include her.

I couldn't wait for the school day to end so I could go home and tell Peter about my progress. But when I finally got home, he didn't give me a chance to tell him about school. He had news for me.

"My mother's coming for her annual disastrous visit," he said, waving a letter around. "Sometime in October."

"What do you mean, disastrous?" I asked. I'd been very curious about Peter's mother but the time never seemed right to ask him. I certainly wasn't going to bring it up with Ben, and the one time I tried to talk to Mom about her, she just shrugged her shoulders and said there was no understanding some people. That's Mom's way of telling me to mind my own business.

"Mom can't deal with me. Dad says it may partly be because she feels guilty about the hemophilia. You could say I got it from her, since that's how you get it. Sons inherit it from their mothers," Peter said. "I can't deal with her either. When things were really bad, she ran off with another

man and left Dad and me. She married him and
moved to Seattle and I stayed here with Dad and
my doctors and my hospital. It was a mess and a
lot of it was my fault. It isn't easy with a kid who's
sick all the time, and I didn't make things any
easier on her. Anyway, she comes here about once
a year, and she tries to make things better, and I
try to make things better, and we usually make
things worse. She leaves in tears and I'm depressed
for a week or two."

"So why are you so happy about it now?" I
asked.

"Because that's just reality," he said. "In my
fantasy version the next visit is always the one
that's going to work. No guilt, no tears. Just good
times. Eventually it's bound to happen."

"I used to not see my father very much," I said.
"When I was in L.A. and he was in New York.
It makes the visits rougher if you don't see them
often."

"Things would be rough between my mother
and me no matter how often we saw each other,"
Peter said. "There are times I really hate her. But
maybe this time will be different."

"I hope so," I said, thinking that I really should
see more of my father. I'd have to give him a call.

"I hope so too," Peter said. "So tell me about
school today. How did things go?"

I gave Peter a rundown, stressing the number of kids I'd spoken with.

"It sounds good," Peter said with great satisfaction when I finished. "Just try not to overdo this star business."

"That's all they wanted to talk about," I said. "Besides, I told everybody I wasn't a star."

"False modesty," he said. "At least that's the way it'll seem. Did anybody seem to hate you?"

"Not that I noticed," I said.

"I wish I knew more about your class," he said. "It sounds like you were talking to a good group of kids, but you can never tell. I want you to be friends with the best."

"You little snob," I said.

"I can afford to be one," he said. "I'm not there."

"It seems to me one of the kids mentioned the class presidency," I said. "I don't think I made that up."

"That sounds promising," he said. "The teachers treating you all right?"

"Everyone except Mr. Taylor, my homeroom teacher. He kept me after homeroom this morning and asked if I'd be trying out for the junior play."

"What did you say?"

"That I didn't know."

"That's a tough one," Peter said. "On the one hand, you don't want to be a show-off. On the other hand, being in the junior play is priceless Americana."

"Peter, the junior play isn't for months," I said. "I've only been in school for a couple of weeks. Can't we wait before we decide?"

"Okay," he said. "Just remind me about it a couple of weeks before auditions."

"Yes, Svengali," I said.

"I'm sorry if I seem pushy," he said. "I guess I am pushy and that's why I seem that way. You're the closest I can get to being normal these days. If things go well for you, then maybe they'll go well for me. Do you understand?"

"I understand," I said. "But I've got to do it on my own too. I can't just make decisions based on what you think. I feel lousy about Anna."

"You'll forget about that in a week," he said. "And you would have paid for it all year. Believe me."

"Just remember," I said, trying to sound firm about it, "you can't lead my life for me."

"I know that," Peter said, looking shocked. "Besides, you're leading my life for me. That's the whole idea."

Chapter
4

Peter had been hoping his mother would come in early October, but she kept sending him notes and telegrams explaining she'd gotten involved in a major real-estate sale, and he could expect her closer to Halloween. Peter claimed it didn't matter, but I could see he was disappointed, so I felt sorry for him. It was easy to feel protective of Peter.

Things were going pretty well at school. Through Cathy and her friends I was getting to know the kids I'd always dreamed of knowing. Class officers, cheerleaders, school paper editors, and honor students. It would have been nice if one of them had asked me out. I had hoped I'd have a date for one of the football games, but I ended up going with some girl friends. Cathy was a cheerleader, and I went to see her. I thought Peter would be eager for all the details but he brushed me off when I started.

"I don't like football," he said.

"Why not?" I asked. I knew he wasn't opposed to sports; he enjoyed baseball and was an avid Yankee fan.

"All that crunching," he said. "I get sick just thinking about it."

So I kept my football anecdotes to myself, although I did tell Peter about how I coached Cathy with her cheers. She did a couple I'd done on *The Kampbell Kids*, so I could give her pointers. Peter approved.

I liked the way things were going that fall. Mom and Ben were obviously happy; Peter was out of the cast and in a wheelchair, spending most of his time out of his bedroom. School was still an adventure, and I liked having friends whose houses I went to and who called me just to chat and not to complain about the next week's script. If this was the life of an average American teen-ager, I liked it. I hadn't started dating yet, but I had the feeling Andy Goodwin was getting ready to ask me out. Andy was class president and he looked a lot like

Barry Cooper. I knew he was really popular and that made me want him more. I was willing to wait.

Peter was, of course, the first to spot trouble ahead. Mom got the *TV Guide* for him on Tuesdays and he read it cover to cover. In the middle of October he noticed that my made-for-TV movie was scheduled for the following Monday.

"Teen-age alcoholic?" he asked me when I got home from school. "Runaway? Prostitute?"

"I wasn't a prostitute," I said indignantly, grabbing the *TV Guide* from him. "Oh, well, maybe just a little bit of one."

"A little bit of a prostitute?" he asked. "Isn't that like being a little pregnant?"

"I was desperate," I said. "You would be too if you had the parents they gave me."

"Oh God," he said. "Next Monday night this epic is going to be on television for everybody to see."

"I should hope so," I said. "They were counting on really high ratings for it."

"You don't take drugs in it, do you?" he asked.

"Just drink," I said. "But alcohol is a drug. They make a really big point of that in the film. All about how I'm addicted. I detox and everything. It was fun."

"Fun?" he shouted.

"After four years of being sweet little Chris

Kampbell? You better believe it. I got to shriek and hallucinate and everything."

"And Angie let you do this?"

"Let her do what?" Mom asked, coming into the living room.

"My movie's going to be on on Monday," I said, handing her the *TV Guide*. "Peter's a little upset that I play a prostitute."

"You weren't exactly a prostitute," she said, handing me back the magazine. "Just a girl in trouble."

"See," I said to Peter.

"I'll say you're in trouble," he said. "Wait until everybody sees this thing. All the work we've done will be for nothing."

"Work?" Mom asked.

"It's only a movie," I said. "It isn't even that, just a big TV show. And the kids are used to seeing me on TV."

"This is different," he said.

"How?" I demanded.

"No braid," he said and wheeled himself back to his bedroom.

I was sure Peter was worrying excessively but just to be on the safe side I didn't talk about the movie. Everybody found out about it though and I had to do a lot of explaining.

"The *TV Guide* exaggerated," I said.

No one believed me, so when people started inviting themselves over to watch the movie with me I turned them all down. I invited Anna instead. Her TV was still broken and unless I asked her, she wouldn't be able to see it. Besides I wanted to show off for her. I was proud of my performance.

"Are you sure it won't ruin your reputation— being seen with me?" she asked.

"I'll take my chances," I said. There were times I could really kill Peter. "Besides, you're the only one in this class I really respect. In terms of artistic judgment, that is. Please come."

"All right," she said. "It should be amusing to see what television is like."

So she came over that Monday night. Peter was in a bad mood anyway, and he sulked when she came in and hardly acknowledged her presence. Of course, Mom and Ben were gracious to her, and Anna chatted with them about school and her parents and the weather. I was too angry at Peter and too nervous about the film to chat with anybody.

Ben turned the set on a couple of minutes before the movie began and fiddled around with the color tones. Before we were quite ready for it there was an announcement that the following show might not be suitable for children and parents should use their discretion.

"Great," Peter said.

And then, there I was, or at least a nineteen-inch version of me, sneaking upstairs to my parents' bedroom closet and taking a swig of Scotch. And for the next two hours I drank, got beaten by my parents, slept in cars, got raped ("I forgot about the rape," Mom said conversationally during a station break), walked the streets (briefly), suffered from D.T.'s, got rescued, sobered up, attended an A.A. meeting, and returned home, only to be confronted once again with my monster parents and the tempting bottle of Scotch. They'd left it open-ended in case the ratings justified making a sequel.

"Well," Ben said when it was finished. He got up and turned off the set.

"You were very good," Mom said. "Very convincing."

"You were excellent," Anna said. "I'm very impressed. I never would have thought, I mean, well, it took me by surprise. How good you were."

"Excellent," Ben said. "A remarkable performance."

"I was good, wasn't I," I said. I love having my work praised.

"Yes, you were," Mom said. "Even the *Times* said you were."

"The *Times* reviewed me?" I asked.

"I didn't want to show you the review beforehand," she said. "They weren't that wild about the whole production, but they said you were remarkably convincing. Here," and she handed me the review.

"'Leigh Thorpe gives a heartrending performance as the troubled teen-ager,'" I read out loud. "'She is convincing every moment of the way, a remarkable accomplishment for such a young actress.'" I read the rest of the review to myself. It was all about how the film was too melodramatic and my redemption, such as it was, too unconvincing. "Not bad," I said, looking at it a second time. "I like the heartrending part."

"I'm surprised the phone isn't ringing," Mom said. "I would have thought all your friends would be watching."

"I'm sure they did," I said. "They probably didn't want to bother us so late at night."

"Ha," Peter said.

We all turned around and looked at him. "Well, Peter?" Ben asked. "What did you think of Leigh's performance?"

"Heartrending," he said and wheeled himself back to his room.

"You have to forgive Peter," Ben said to Anna. "He tires very easily."

"I understand," she said. "As a matter of fact, I'm kind of tired too. That was a very draining experience, and I do have school tomorrow."

I walked her to the door. "It's a crime you've given up acting," she said as she turned to leave. "Wasting talent like that on a school like ours. You should be doing theater. Juliet."

"I'm not quite ready for Shakespeare yet," I said, blushing.

"You're not ready for average American kids yet either," she said. "Good-night."

"You should have an exciting day at school tomorrow," Mom said as she started straightening the room up.

"That's for sure," I said, trying to calculate the odds of my coming down with pneumonia before the alarm went off. They didn't seem good. I said good-night to Ben and Mom and went into Peter's room to hear the worst.

"It's not your fault," he said. He was already in bed, surrounded by books.

"That's a comfort," I said. "How bad do you think it's going to be?"

"It's hard to say," he replied. "You weren't a prostitute for very long. I just wish you hadn't cut your hair before making it," he said. "You look just like that character."

"Of course I do," I said.

"You don't look that much like Chris Kampbell anymore," he said. "I don't know. Maybe nobody will have seen it. Maybe everybody'll think it's funny."

"You think it's going to be awful, don't you," I said.

"I think it's a major setback," he said. "But it may not be fatal."

I wasn't very comforted but I knew sticking around wouldn't help, so I went to bed. I dreamed I won all kinds of awards for my performance but couldn't pick up any of them because all my friends were laughing at me. I've had more restful nights' sleeps.

I could tell from the looks I got as soon as I approached the high school that things were going to be just awful. Mr. Taylor, my homeroom teacher, didn't help matters any.

"I hope all of you saw *Mary's Story* last night," he said. "Our own Leigh Thorpe starred in it and in my opinion gave a truly brilliant performance."

I blushed and thought about slugging him. I'd never wanted to hit anyone who'd liked my work before.

"The movie was a bit too melodramatic for my tastes," he continued. "But I was very impressed by Leigh's performance. I can only continue to hope she'll agree to appear in our junior class play."

The bell rang for first period. I gathered my books together and made my way out of the room. Most of the kids who usually said hi to me ignored me, and the rest of the school stared straight at me. I thought about lurching around a bit but I only stood more stiffly and walked straight ahead. Nobody came up to me during any of my morning classes to say they'd seen the show. Instead they whispered to each other while I tried to keep my cheeks from burning. The only direct contact I had with anyone was with a boy I didn't know who whispered, "Hey, pussy" at me. Just what I didn't need.

After a morning of whispers and funny looks I started getting very upset. So while we were changing after gym, I asked Anna to have lunch with me. I didn't want to face everyone alone.

"But I thought you ate with your friends," she said. "The all-American gang."

"So eat with all of us," I said. "I don't know how they're going to react."

"All right," she said after thinking about it. "Someone has to protect you from yourself."

We deliberately lingered before joining the others for lunch. I'd gotten into the habit of eating with Cathy, Andy, Bob, and Sharon. I sensed a difference in their attitudes toward me, but I didn't know whether it was because of the movie or because I'd deliberately foisted Anna on them.

"That was quite some movie," Sharon said as I unwrapped my sandwich.

"Thank you," I said.

"It was very well acted," Cathy said.

I gave Anna a quick desperate look. "Tell me," she said brightly. "What do you people think about Eurocommunism?"

"It'll never last," Andy said. "Frankly, Leigh, I was a little surprised you'd be in something like that."

"Why?" I asked. Oh, what was perfect Andy going to say to me?

"This may sound very old-fashioned," he said, "but I think there are some things that just don't belong on television."

"I personally find Eurocommunism fascinating," Anna said. "So enigmatic."

I didn't know who I wanted to kill first. "What shouldn't be on TV?" I said. Eurocommunism could wait.

"Movies that glorify delinquency," Andy said.

"Glorify?" I said. "I *suffered* straight through that thing."

"Even your suffering was glamorous," he said.

"And you stopped drinking too easily if you ask me."

"What do you know about it?" I asked. "Are you an alcoholic?"

"I could ask you the same thing," he said.

I was stunned.

"Leigh is an actress," Anna said coolly. "She was acting. She was given lines and direction and gave a performance."

"That's right," Cathy said. "That's like saying if somebody plays a Nazi, he is one."

"I'm not saying Leigh is an alcoholic," Andy said. "What I am saying is that I was disappointed in her choice of material."

"It was a good part," I said. "And I did a good job."

"I agree," Bob said. "I thought Leigh was excellent."

"She certainly was," Anna said. "But Andy has an interesting point too. Perhaps there ought to be some form of control over what appears on television."

We all looked at her.

"I'm probably not the one to talk about it," she said. "Since our TV set's been broken for five years. But . . ."

"You never watch television at all?" Sharon asked.

"No," Anna said. "Before last night I don't think I've seen anything on television for the last five years."

"Really?" Cathy said. "That's incredible. What do you do evenings?"

"I read a lot," Anna said. "And I play the piano. And I cook—and do my homework of course. I keep busy."

"That's great," Cathy said. "We tried keeping the TV off for a week last year and we just couldn't do it. Of course, I have two younger brothers and they had to watch the cartoons. They were unbearable."

"I can't imagine life without television," Sharon said.

I cast a quick look at Andy. He was still very angry. But so was I, angry at him and his close-minded, ignorant ways. I was grateful to Anna too, for finally, successfully changing the subject. But still just about ready to kill Andy.

Didn't he realize what perfect dates we could have? How could he blow such glorious perfection with a small mind and big mouth?

Chapter
5

I spent the next few days waiting for Andy to come to his senses, which he chose not to do. Perfect date or not, I was losing patience. And the whispering and dirty comments persisted as well. It was one awful week.

Peter, on the other hand, was very nice to me. He was angry about the lousy way the boys were acting and gave me advice on how to handle it: ignore them. Which I did.

"I'd help if I could," he said. "But I'd be a rotten bodyguard."

It wasn't my body I feared for, but my nerves, which were on the verge of shattering. I didn't want Mom or Ben to know things were less than perfect, so I couldn't talk to them. I felt an almost irrational impulse to confide my troubles in my father, who was currently playing Lefty O'Roarke on *Joys and Sorrows* in New York, and on Friday when he called to congratulate me for my performance I asked if I could spend the weekend with him, but he was busy, which didn't help my ego any.

And even though I knew it was silly, I was a little bit hurt that nobody I knew from the business had bothered to call. I had been good in the part, and if I'd been in L.A., people would have let me know how much they'd liked it. But now that I was stuck out on Long Island, nobody felt it was worth the long-distance call. Everybody I didn't want to react to the movie did, and everybody I wanted to ignored it. Life stank.

I was telling Peter most of this that Friday night when my mother knocked on his bedroom door and came in. "There's a phone call for you, Peter," she said, not sounding particularly happy about it.

We'd heard the phone ring a few minutes before but had ignored it. "Who is it?" he asked Mom.

"Your mother," she said and left the room.

I made a move to leave, but Peter gestured that I should stay where I was. He picked up his extension and said "Hi, Mom."

They talked for a few minutes while I was sitting there trying to listen and not listen simultaneously. Peter seemed cheerful and when he hung up he told me his mother was in New York and would be over the next day to see him.

"That's great," I said, not meaning it. I felt very ill at ease about the whole thing.

Peter insisted on going out to the living room to tell his father about the visit, so I helped him into his wheelchair and we went. Ben was pacing from one end of the room to the other, and Mom had her "there there" expression on her face. I recognized it from all the times I'd tried out for parts that I didn't get.

"That was Mom," Peter said brightly.

"Yes, I know," Ben said. "What does she want?"

"The pleasure of my company," Peter said. "She's coming tomorrow morning. Nine or ten, she said."

"Have you forgotten you have a doctor's appointment tomorrow morning?" Ben asked.

"You know, I did forget," Peter said. "Oh, well, I'm sure Doctor Loeb won't mind changing the appointment. Mom's come all the way from Seattle just to see me. That's got to take first priority."

"I'm sure if you called and explained, she'd come later in the day," Ben said.

"But I don't want to," Peter said. "I want to see her. I can see Dr. Loeb next week."

"It'll just upset you to see your mother," Ben said. "It always does. I don't see why you're so eager to see her."

"Because she's my mother, dammit," Peter said. "Besides I'm older now."

"Of course you're older. She only sees you once a year."

"Exactly," Peter said. "And that's why it's more important to me to see her than to go to the doctor. God knows, I see him more than once a year."

"I'll call Dr. Loeb and change the appointment," Mom said.

"Thank you," Peter said. "Dad, will you be here tomorrow when Mom comes?"

"I'm not as crazy as you are," Ben said. "I'll be out playing tennis."

Ben loved playing tennis; I knew that from his L.A. visits. But he rarely played when he was home, preferring to spend his weekends with Peter. He would have been the one to take Peter to his doctor's appointment, so this tennis playing business was definitely intended as a slap in the face. I marveled at just how awful parents could be.

"Fine," Mom said. The tennis must have been as big a surprise to her as to the rest of us, but she's used to temperament. "You go play tennis tomorrow and I'll play hostess to Margaret. Leigh, do you have any plans?"

I sure didn't, but I looked at Peter for a clue.

"Leigh, stay here and meet Mom?" he said. "I'd like the two of you to meet."

"Sure," I said. "I'd like to."

"That's all settled then," Mom said. "Does anybody care to watch TV?"

"No thanks, Angie," Peter said. "I think I'm going to go to bed now, so I'll be rested for tomorrow." He wheeled himself out of the room.

I stared after him, trying to figure out how I too could disappear tactfully. The last place I wanted to be was with Ben, who was clearly ready to explode. "I have homework to do," I said, which on a Friday night sounded pretty silly. Fortunately everybody was upset enough not to notice, so I left. I really wished that my father hadn't been too busy to see me.

I don't know what time Ben left the next morning, but he was gone by the time I got up, and I got up at eight because Peter was up and making a lot of noise. So was Mom, who was vacuuming frantically when I found her in the living room.

"The house is spotless," I told her. Mom keeps a very clean house.

"This is Ben's ex-wife," Mom said and turned the vacuum cleaner back on. "Is that what you're planning to wear?"

I was wearing a T-shirt and jeans. "What's wrong?" I asked.

"Peter's mother is coming to visit," she said. "Don't you think you should make a little effort to look nice?"

Ben's ex-wife, Peter's mother. She sure seemed to require a lot of effort from the two of us. "Honestly," I said to Mom, and then I thought about how excited Peter was about this visit. Also, Mom looked ready to kill and I wasn't eager to be her victim. "All right," I said and went back to my bedroom, where I put on my neatest, most conservative skirt and blouse. I debated about putting on makeup and decided against it. I felt like I was meeting my future mother-in-law.

Peter didn't seem too concerned when his mother hadn't shown by eleven o'clock. By twelve, Peter was still calm but I was a nervous wreck. When the phone rang I jumped a straight six feet in the air.

Mom called Peter to the phone. I sat in the living room and seriously considered taking up nail biting.

"That was my mother," he told me when he came back in. "She's running a little late. She missed her connections."

She'd be missing a few teeth if she didn't show up soon, I thought. I smiled at Peter and mumbled something about how easy it was to miss a train.

By two, I was getting increasingly nervous about the possibility that Ben would show up before Margaret did. I wasn't sure but I had the feeling that he was the "I told you so" type. I wondered whether Mom had called Ben and told him what was going on, but I didn't want to ask in front of Peter. And he was staying out in the living room waiting for his mother.

"She'll be here any minute," he said at two fifteen.

Almost as though she'd heard her cue, Margaret rang the bell. Mom was in the kitchen, so I opened the door.

By that point I was expecting some kind of monster, so the small, well-dressed woman outside startled me. "Hello," she said. "Is Peter here? I'm his mother."

"Yes, certainly," I said. "Come in. I'm Leigh, Peter's stepsister."

"Hello, Leigh," she said. "Peter's written all about you."

I smiled. Margaret spotted Peter in the living

room and walked over to him. She paused for a moment, then bent down and kissed him.

"I'm sorry I'm late, darling," she said. "I missed the twelve-o-two train by just one minute."

"I thought you were going to be here this morning," Peter said. "Of course I also thought you were going to be here three weeks ago."

"I would have been if I could," she said. She stood there for a moment, then took a deep breath and took off her coat. I took it immediately and hung it in the closet.

"Thank you," she called to me. I stood in the doorway and debated whether to go back in. I figured if I was wanted they'd know where to find me, so I stayed where I was.

"How are you feeling?" Margaret asked Peter.

"Okay," Peter said, shrugging his shoulders. "And you?"

"I'm fine," she said. "Don sends his love."

"Thank you," Peter said. "Give him my regards."

There was an achingly long silence. "Well," Margaret finally said. "Are you keeping up with your physical therapy?"

"Yeah," Peter said.

"But you'd rather read," his mother said. "Or play chess. Or watch TV."

"Of course I would," Peter said. "Physical therapy is painful."

"But you'll never get well without it," she said.

"Mom, I'm never going to get well," Peter said. "Not really."

"Don't you think I know that?" she said.

"Yes, of course," Peter said. "I'm sorry."

"I'm sorry too," she said. "I'm not in the house ten seconds before I'm ordering you around. Just like old times."

"How are things in Seattle?" Peter asked. "How's your job going?"

"Fine," Margaret said. "Real estate has its ups and downs, but right now I'm keeping very busy with it."

"Making a lot of sales?"

"Enough," she said. "And you?"

"I'm not making any sales," he said.

"That wasn't what I meant," Margaret said.

"Forgive me," Peter said. "I thought a little humor might help."

"Humor," Margaret said. "Yes, I suppose it would help."

"Yes," Peter said.

Another pause. "Peter darling, you know how nervous I get before one of these visits," Margaret said. "It isn't easy when you only see your son once a year. I worry we won't have anything to talk about, that you won't really be glad to see me."

"I'm not a monster, Mom," Peter said.

"I'm not either. Really I'm not," she said, then took a deep breath. "So tell me, are things cheerier for you now that you have Leigh as a companion?"

"A little playmate, you mean?" Peter asked. "Only this one is live-in, so she can't possibly escape?"

I cleared my throat. "Excuse me," I said as brightly as possible. "I'll be in the kitchen if you need me."

"No, Leigh, wait a minute," Margaret said. "Leigh, I don't know what Peter's told you about me, but I really do love him."

"Of course," I said. "He never said you didn't."

"It's just so hard . . . we see each other so rarely," she said. "Perhaps if you joined us, if the three of us talked for a while, it might be easier. Couldn't you sit down with us? Just for a little while?"

"Oh, no," I said. "You and Peter have so much to catch up with, and I just know my mother needs me. I really ought to help her out."

"I only hoped . . ." Margaret said.

"Let her go," Peter said. "Go on, Leigh. We'll see you later."

"Thanks, Peter," I said and went to the kitchen, hoping to find Mom calm and normal. Instead I saw she was sitting by the kitchen table, crying softly. I ran over to her. "Mom, what is it?" I asked.

She shook her head, blew her nose, and said, "I'm all right. Really."

"What's the matter?" I persisted.

"Sometimes it's just too much for me," she said softly. "Peter's wound up tighter than a clock and Ben is nowhere to be found and who's around to pick up the pieces? Me. You and me. It isn't fair."

"It isn't," I said, sitting down next to her. "Especially not for you."

"Or you either," Mom said. "This has nothing to do with us. It's their problem, Ben's and Margaret's, and Ben is refusing to handle it. No, that's not true. He's deliberately making it worse."

"It's a mess," I agreed.

"She comes once a year," Mom whispered angrily. "Once a goddamn year, and she stays for ten minutes . . ."

"Oh, I hope so," I said.

Mom smiled. "With luck, for ten minutes, and then she vanishes and isn't heard from again for another year. If you only knew the things Ben's told me about her."

"Ben can't be too objective about her," I said.

Mom ignored me. "Let's go out for a walk," she

said. "Or shopping. Let's go shopping. We haven't gone shopping together in so long."

"Should we?" I asked.

"Probably not," she said. "Let's do it anyway. "We'll both buy new dresses."

"All right," I said, as eager as she was to get out of the house. "Wait until I get my bag."

"I'll meet you in the living room," Mom said.

I cut through the living room as inconspicuously as I could and got my pocketbook. Sure enough, Mom was in the living room chatting with Peter and Margaret when I got back.

"We should be home before supper," Mom said to them. "Have a nice visit."

"We will," Peter said grimly. I wanted to hug him but instead I said good-bye and Mom and I left.

I've had better shopping trips with Mom, but I've had worse too. We each bought two dresses, one pair of shoes, and some overpriced night-gowns. In addition, we treated ourselves to hot fudge sundaes and I bought a Barry Cooper fan magazine in the hope (gratified) that it might have some pictures of me in it. I looked good with a braid.

We stayed out for over three hours. When we got back Margaret was gone and Ben still hadn't returned. Peter was in the living room, still looking grim.

"Too much for you, huh," he said to Mom and me.

"Peter, I'm sorry," Mom said. "But I thought your visit might go better if Leigh and I were gone. If you and your mother had some privacy."

"Yeah, sure," Peter said.

"How long did she stay?" I asked, feeling very guilty for having run out.

"She left about an hour ago," he said. "She had a train to catch."

"Will she be seeing you again?" Mom asked.

"I don't think so," Peter said. "Look, if it's okay with you, I think I'll skip supper. I don't feel too well."

"You didn't have any lunch," Mom said. "You shouldn't miss so many meals."

"I'll live," he said and left the living room. Mom and I stared at each other.

"I didn't think he'd be alone," she said defensively. "I thought Margaret would stay until we got back or Ben would be home by now. It never occurred to me."

"He'll be okay," I said. "I'll go in there and talk with him."

"Would you?" Mom asked gratefully. "I don't want Ben to come home and find Peter like this."

I kissed Mom and went into Peter's room. He was lying on his bed staring at the ceiling.

"All right," I said. "What's going on?"

"Nothing," he said, not looking at me.

"Do you want your father to find you like this?" I asked. "He'll never let you see your mother."

"Great loss," he said.

There was no point trying to make Peter talk if he didn't want to. So I just sighed and said, "God, what a lousy week."

"They happen," Peter said. "Is Angie upset?"

"Of course," I said. "Do you think you could come out and make things a little easier?"

He hesitated for a moment. "I really don't feel well," he said. "But why not? Hiding in here isn't going to make things any better."

I helped him out of bed and noticed that he winced as he got into his chair. "Are you okay?" I asked.

"I'm fine," he said. "Come on, let's put on a cheery face." He grinned, looking remarkably silly. So I made a funny face at him and we went back out.

Ben came home a few minutes later, claiming to feel fine. Peter claimed the same thing. We had a late supper and chatted about various meaningless things. We watched some TV and then Peter excused himself and went to bed. Ben turned to Mom

75

and me and asked how Margaret's visit had gone. We explained we hadn't been home for most of it, leaving out all the pertinent details.

I went to bed around midnight and it took me awhile to fall asleep. When I heard the sounds of people moving around, I thought at first I was still sleeping, but the noise was loud enough to wake me. It was about three A.M. I thought about hiding in my room for a while longer, sighed, put on my robe, and, eyes blinking as they adjusted to the light, made my way out into the hall.

"What's going on?" I asked Mom, glad I'd run into her and not Ben.

"Peter's in a lot of pain," she said. "Ben's giving him a transfusion."

"It's not serious, is it?" I asked, trying to remember what Peter had told me.

"Of course it's serious," Mom said. "It's always serious."

"Have you called the doctor?" I asked.

Mom nodded. "He said 'Take two transfusions and call me in the morning,'" she said.

"Mom!" I said.

"I'm not kidding," she said. "We're to try to make it through the night, and if the bleeding doesn't stop or if it gets worse, we call him and he calls the hospital."

I could hear Peter groaning. I really wanted to

hide then. I'm not very good with pain, and even though I'd known there were times when Peter wasn't feeling well, he deliberately never made a fuss.

Ben came out before I had a chance to run back to my bedroom. "Leigh," he said, his eyes lighting when he saw me. "Just what the doctor ordered."

"What can I do?" I asked.

"You can keep Peter distracted," he said. "If he has something other than the pain to think about he'll feel better."

"Okay," I said and went straight into Peter's room. I just plowed in there; if I'd taken a moment to think or ask questions, I never would have gone in.

"Hi there," I said without even looking at him. "You woke me."

He looked pale and feverish, with sweat pouring out. He looked at me and groaned.

"So I don't look great at three in the morning," I said, trying to sound normal. "You don't look so hot yourself." I moved over to sit down on the bed next to him.

"No!" he cried. "Not on the bed."

"I must look worse than I thought," I said. I was shaking, so I took a deep breath and sat on the chair instead. "So, have you read any good books lately?"

Peter managed a little laugh.

"Did I tell you Mr. Taylor's still after me to be in the junior play?" I asked. "What do you think?"

"I think I'm going to die," he said.

Just what I needed to hear. "And miss my Long Island debut?" I asked, my voice cracking. I dug my fingernails into my palm. The pain calmed me slightly.

"Leigh, I don't feel like talking," Peter said.

"Do you realize it's only midnight out on the coast?" I asked brightly. "People are probably out at parties right now. Barry Cooper loves going to parties."

"Thrillsville," Peter muttered.

I giggled. He was starting to sound almost normal. "I didn't get invited to many, on account of my wholesome image," I said. "Hey, maybe we should give a party?"

"A party?" Peter asked, turning his head to see me better. He moaned as he moved.

"Sure," I said. "Maybe at Thanksgiving. Ten kids? Does that sound about right?"

"I don't know," he said.

"I think so," I said. "I'll ask Cathy for advice. But I'm definitely inviting Anna, whether you like it or not."

"Mistake," he said.

"It is not," I said. "Anna isn't exactly intimate

with the other kids, but she has lunch with us every day now. And the other kids think she's kind of funny. Except for David Marx. He thinks she's a challenge. Only she won't give him the time of day because he's only seventeen. Anna refuses to consider men under the age of thirty."

"What kind of music?" Peter asked.

"I don't know," I said. "Records, I guess. And I could ask Andy to bring his guitar. I know he plays."

"I used to play," Peter said. He looked almost interested.

"You did?" I said. "I didn't know that."

"I haven't played in a while," he said. "But maybe if I practiced between now and Thanksgiving . . ."

Two sentences in a row. I felt like giving myself a Nobel prize in Medicine.

"That would be great," I said.

"Do you sing?" he asked. "You did on the show."

"I sing terribly," I said. "The second year they decided we should all sing, so they made us all try, and I was just awful."

"Were you dubbed?" he asked.

"No more than anybody else," I said. "We were all amplified a bit. They gave most of the solos to Barry, of course, and they gave Natalie Collins a few. She had a really pretty voice."

"What did you do if you couldn't sing?" Peter asked.

"I hummed," I said. "Whenever they needed harmony, there I was humming. I'm a great hummer."

Peter laughed. Maybe not a hearty laugh, but a laugh nonetheless. "I'll play, you'll hum," he said. "I'll play *The Bridge on the River Kwai.*"

"I can hum songs with words," I said indignantly. "I have a lot of self-discipline."

"I'll have to get my guitar out," Peter said. "I'll start practicing Monday, when you're in school so it won't bother you."

"Won't your tutor mind?" I asked.

"Jim? No, he plays the guitar too. I'll ask him for some help."

"Great," I said. "How old is he anyway?"

"In his twenties," Peter said. "Why?"

"He's too young for Anna," I said. "But maybe we should invite him anyway and see if sparks fly."

"I think he's married," Peter said.

"Anna wouldn't mind," I said. "How do you feel?"

"Better," he said.

"Are you going to keep groaning and make us all miserable?" I asked. "Or are you going to let us sleep?"

"I'll try to keep down to a low groan," he said.

"Good," I said. "Do you want me to stay awhile longer?"

"Would you?" he asked. "You don't have to talk. Just sit here and look cheerful."

"Sure," I said. I sat still for a few moments, until the silence seemed oppressive to me. Then I started humming.

Peter laughed at first, then he hummed along. We hummed most of the top ten songs and then worked our way through various Beatles classics. Eventually he stopped humming and I lowered my volume, hoping he was falling asleep.

When I thought it was safe to, I stopped humming and got up to leave the room. I tiptoed out and had just made it to the door when I heard Peter's voice. He sounded half-asleep.

"How about some Rolling Stones?" he mumbled.

I tried not to laugh too loud. "Try to sleep," I said. "Give a poor innocent bystander some peace."

"Okay," he mumbled and started breathing deeply and peacefully. I opened the door and left the room.

"So what about that party you promised me?" Peter said the next afternoon when I went into his room to check on him. He still looked pale but he was obviously feeling better.

"Party," I said. "I didn't realize you'd remember."

"Of course I remember," he said. "Why shouldn't I?"

"You were half out of your mind with pain," I said.

"The other half of my mind remembered," he said. "When should we give it? Next Saturday?"

"Will you be out of bed by next Saturday?" I asked.

"That's a good question," he said. "Okay, two Saturdays. I'll be better by then."

"Just out of bed," I said. "And giving a party. Your father will love that."

"I can handle Dad," Peter said. "Two weeks then."

"No, wait a second," I said. "What's the big deal about giving a party anyway?"

"I don't know," Peter said. "You tell me."

"What?"

"You're the one who keeps coming up with objections," he said. "What's the big deal?"

I scowled.

"How many guesses do I get?" Peter said.

"It's just I've never given a party before," I said. "Not really."

"You're not going to tell me you never had a party," Peter said.

"No, of course not," I said. "I had parties. But they were different."

"How?"

"There were photographers there," I said. "And I had to invite all the other Kampbell Kids, even though I hated half of them. And the parties were always elaborate. Real bands. Fancy cakes. I gave a party when we had our first gold record. Mom did all the arranging. We had a cake shaped like a gold record. It tasted awful too."

"Real bands," Peter said. "That sounds good."

"It was horrible," I said. "They were all horrible. I hardly knew most of the kids there and there were hundreds of them. I'm exaggerating, but they were big, big parties and we all had to dress up and look our best and be wholesome. Can you imagine a party when you have to look good and wholesome at the same time? It was awful."

"But our party won't be anything like that," Peter said. "It'll just be a few kids and no photographers and we can all look rotten if you'd like."

"But I never gave a party like that," I said. "I don't know how. And if you're in bed you won't be much help."

"Didn't Chris Kampbell give parties?" Peter asked.

I thought about it. "Pajama parties," I said. "I was always hot for those. But Cathy Kampbell used to give parties, which I always wanted to go to, but she said I was too young."

"What were those parties like?"

"A few kids," I said. "Potato chips. Records."

"Then we'll give a party like that," Peter said. "Okay?"

"Can we wait a little while?" I asked. "At least until you're out of bed for a while?"

"Why?"

"Maybe I'll get invited to a few parties in the meantime," I said. "I might even have a date. Greater miracles have happened."

"What do you need a date for?" Peter said. "Lots of people go to parties without dates. Even I used to. Last one I went to I got a nosebleed and I thought my friend's mother would drop dead on the spot."

"What happened?" I asked.

"Nobody died," he said. "Okay, we'll wait a little while. Dad'll be happier about it if we do anyway."

"Thanks," I said. "I promise when we give it, it'll be one fine party."

Chapter 6

I'd managed to forget the junior play by the time Mr. Taylor announced his selection in early November.

"We're doing something a little meatier than usual," he said, staring straight at me. I had the uncomfortable feeling that I was the ˈmeat. "*Antigone*, by Jean Anouilh."

There was a buzzing around the homeroom.

"The announcement for auditions will be on the loudspeaker in a day or so," he continued. "But I thought I'd give my homeroomers early notice. Inspire a few of them, I hope, to audition for us."

I managed a sickly smile and tried to avoid eye contact. It didn't help, for when I was leaving the classroom Mr. Taylor stopped me. "You'd make an inspiring Antigone," he said. "I admit I chose the play with you in mind."

"Thank you," I said, trying to worm my way out of there. "I'll have to read the play and see."

"A professional!" he cried. "I bet you're the only student who's even thought to read the play first."

"Force of habit," I said. "Now if you'll excuse me . . ."

So at lunch I ate my sandwich hastily, excused myself from the crowd, and went up to the library, where I requested and received a copy of the play. I read most of the first act, which was more than enough to convince me what an awful Antigone I'd make. The play might have been written in the twentieth century, but it was all very Greek tragic and alien to me. I left it there, so if anybody else displayed professional tendencies it would be there for them to read.

"I can't possibly do it," I told Peter that afternoon.

"I think you ought to," he said.

I ignored him. "First of all, I'm totally miscast," I said. "Antigone is spunky. Spunk is just one of those things I can't act."

"Oh, come on," he said. "Even if you can't do

spunk on a professional level, you'd still be head and shoulders above everybody else in the cast."

"That's the other thing," I said. "I'll make everybody else look bad, which, believe it or not, will not make me look good in comparison. Just show-offy. And I'd be so bored."

"Everybody's going to think you're a real snob if you don't at least try out," Peter said.

"If I try out, Taylor'll cast me," I said. "He practically offered me a contract."

"That's what I mean," he said. "If you aren't in the show people'll think you think you're too good for it."

"But I am," I said.

"That may be," Peter said. "But you're going to lose points if you don't do it."

"In the long run I'll lose points if I do," I said. "There'll be kids who resent me for trying out too, you know. Kids who'll be jealous. Not to mention the points I'll lose when I punch Mr. Taylor in the mouth. Which I'll be bound to do at some point during rehearsals."

"Sure, some kids will be jealous," Peter said. "But if you aren't in the show most of the kids'll think you're letting them down. Or putting them down, which is worse."

"Let them think whatever they want," I said, starting to get angry. "My decision is final."

"Your decision is crazy," he said.

"Only because you don't agree with it."

"I don't agree with it because you're all wrong," he said. "And you know it."

"I do not know it, because I don't agree with you," I said. "Honestly, Peter, you can be such a manipulative little dictator at times."

"Manipulative?" he said, his eyes flashing. "Dictator? I thought we both wanted the same thing."

"We do," I said. "But you think it has to be done your way or not at all."

"When I'm right, yes, I think it should be done my way," he said. "And haven't I been right more often than not?"

"You were all wrong about Anna," I said. "You said she'd never fit in and she does. She has lunch with all of us every day and she doesn't spit at anybody. At least not so you'd notice."

Peter stared at me for a moment, then broke down and grinned. "I'd like to see somebody spit subtly," he said.

"I'll bring her over for a demonstration," I said. "Peter, I'm not doing the play."

"So I gathered," he said. "Okay, what are you going to tell the other kids?"

"That I don't think it would be fair," I said. "And that I hate the idea of working with Mr. Taylor."

Peter nodded. "That's probably your best bet," he said. "Nothing about being miscast though. Or being bored."

"I'm not that dumb," I said.

"You're not dumb at all," he said. "Just pig-headed and obnoxious."

"Why, Peter," I said. "I didn't know you cared."

"I'm good at keeping my feelings secret," he said. I wasn't sure anymore that he was joking. I didn't feel like talking seriously, especially not right after a fight, so I excused myself and went into the kitchen to help Mom with supper.

The next day at lunch I told the kids that I'd given it a lot of thought and had decided against trying out.

"I think you're right," Anna said after I explained my on-the-record reasons. "Besides, you're miscast."

It took me a moment before I realized just who Anna regarded as being perfectly cast in the part. Then I smiled.

"I think you should try out," Cathy said. "We'd bring in so much more money if you're in the show."

"The junior play always sells out anyway," Andy said. "And they won't let us do more than two shows, so Leigh's presence wouldn't really affect it."

89

"But we could charge more money for the tickets," Cathy said. "Or maybe we could enter one of those contests for best high school production."

"That really wouldn't be fair," Anna said. "Our school would have the benefit of a professional in the lead role."

I loved the way Anna was defending my position. Very spunky of her.

"I'm not going to do it and that's final," I said. "So don't give me a bad time, okay? I'm going to have to deal with Taylor's heartbreak all year as it is."

"Why can't you work on one of the committees," Sharon said. "Props or costumes or publicity. I bet you'd be great on publicity."

"Oh, no," I said. "I don't do that. I'm an actress."

I was greeted by a tableful of funny stares.

"The play will be fine without me," I said hastily. "And I'll be in the audience cheering everybody on. I'm a great audience, really."

Anna snickered, but Cathy mercifully changed the subject and I found myself rescued from the bear trap of my own making.

The next morning I put Mr. Taylor out of his misery fast by telling him I wasn't going to try out. Not showing up at auditions was the coward's way of doing it, I had decided. Peter had opted for cowardice, but I had a nagging fear that Taylor wouldn't hold the auditions if he didn't find me there. So I told him.

"I'm very disappointed," he said. "Not only because I was looking forward to working with you, but because I thought you had fit in very nicely in our little school."

"It just wouldn't be fair," I said.

"I shouldn't admit this, but I'd given you the part of Antigone already," he said. "All you would have had to do was show up at auditions and the part was yours."

"I appreciate it," I said. "And it would have been a pleasure working with you, but I just don't think I should."

"Student director then?" he asked. "I'd give you more responsibility than the student director usually has, of course."

"Oh, no, no thank you," I said.

His eyes lit up. "Understudy," he said. "A show this complex certainly needs one."

I had an image of some poor girl being pushed down the stairs right before opening night just so the understudy would have a chance. I shuddered and said I really couldn't.

"You're being very uncooperative," he said. "Were you always this difficult to work with?"

"Worse," I lied cheerfully. "I'm really a monster when I'm acting. My directors hated me."

"I can see why," he said. "I'm sure it would have been a very educational experience for both of us, but I can see your mind is made up."

"It is," I said.

"Very well," he said. "I trust you'll at least see our little production."

"I wouldn't miss it," I said. "Now I really have to go."

"Certainly," he said. "I also have a great deal of work to do before the rehearsals begin. Very well, Leigh. You are excused."

I smiled politely and walked as rapidly as possible out of there. Going to high school certainly was complicated.

Much to my delight, Anna was cast as Antigone.

"I'm surprised you even tried out," I said, teasing her after the casting had been announced. "Bothering yourself with a mere high school play."

"If it had been the standard fare I wouldn't have," she said. "*Arsenic and Old Lace*, that sort of thing. But how could I pass up a chance to do *Antigone*?"

"You'll be great," I said. "Very regal."

"Can you help me with the part?" she asked.

I thought about it. "I won't help you with interpretation," I said. "That's between you and Mr.

Taylor. But I can show you some stuff about being on stage that might help."

"Thank you," she said. "I'm really very nervous."

"It'll be my pleasure," I said, and it turned out it was. I enjoyed teaching Anna tricks of the trade. We did relaxing exercises together and I helped her with stage posture. She came over almost every day after rehearsal and we worked together. Cathy and Andy also had parts in the play and they came over a couple of times as well. I felt as if I was holding rehearsals in exile, but Mr. Taylor didn't seem to mind and I enjoyed the contact with acting. And Andy seemed to warm up to me when we were working together. He smiled a lot more at me and I started hoping again he'd ask me out.

"It was good of you not to audition," he said to me one afternoon. "You let Anna have a chance."

"Thank you," I said. I guessed the trick with Andy was not to act. That would be simple enough. I was retired after all. I just hoped he asked me out before I started getting Social Security.

Peter was a little concerned still that my friendship with Anna might adversely affect me in school, but he shouldn't have worried. Now that Anna was playing Antigone, she was a certified class genius, however eccentric. She still let everybody know exactly what she thought about

Madison High School, but nobody seemed to mind. As a matter of fact, a lot of times other kids agreed with her.

"It is dull sometimes," Cathy said to me after school one day. "I only wish I could get into New York more often."

I was dumbfounded. I hadn't been in New York since I got off the airplane from L.A. I supposed it was nice having New York nearby, in case I felt an attack of culturitis, but for the time being I was quite content with suburbia. I even felt a little betrayed by Cathy's cavalier rejection of everything I held sacred.

"You don't really think it's dull here, do you?" I asked her. "I thought you liked it here."

"I do," she said. "But it is dull sometimes. Always the same kids and the same activities. You don't know what a godsend you were. The first interesting thing to happen here in years."

"But cheerleading," I said. "The school play. All the clubs you belong to."

"They're fun," she said. "But they're not everything. Honestly, Leigh. I may not be as sophisticated as Anna, but I'm not brainless either. I like rock concerts and theater and seeing movies with subtitles. I love the ballet. Lots of things like that."

"Does everybody feel like you?" I asked. "Bored and frustrated?"

"Now look," she said. "I didn't say I felt bored and frustrated. I like what I'm doing and where I am. I just said I wished I could get into New York more often. And yeah, a lot of the kids wish they could too. And some are bored and frustrated."

"Oh," I said. I still couldn't really believe anybody could be bored and frustrated and be a cheerleader too.

"You coming to the play opening night?" she asked. The play had been in rehearsal for three weeks and was due to open the first Friday in December.

"I wouldn't miss it," I said. "It's the high point of my social calendar."

"I believe you," Cathy said. "You sure are gung-ho for the simple life."

"Come on, Cathy," I said. "I get enough of that stuff from Anna."

"Okay," she said and grinned. "It's just that you're fun to tease."

"Yeah?" I said, feeling pleased.

"Yeah," she said. "You coming with a date?"

"You must be kidding," I said. "Maybe I'll ask Peter."

"Peter?" Cathy asked. "Is he well enough?"

"Yeah, I think so," I said. "One evening out won't kill him."

"You shouldn't make jokes like that," she said.

"I wasn't joking," I said. "He's okay enough to go out once in a while. It would be good for him."

"Peter's cute," Cathy said.

"He is?" I said. "I never really thought about it."

"You're practically brother and sister," she said. "Is he always going to be an invalid?"

"No," I said. "He's never exactly going to be healthy, but he'll get better."

"I think he's so brave," she said. "The way he suffers so silently."

"He doesn't like to make a fuss," I said. "I guess he is brave."

"I hope he can come to the play," Cathy said. "If he gets out maybe he'll start to date."

"There's that word again," I said. "Peter better not start dating before I do. I'd kill him."

"You're so noble and unselfish," Cathy said. "An inspiration to us all."

I would have slugged her but I liked the idea that I was fun to tease, so I just smiled.

Peter was delighted to take me to the play and I was delighted to have an escort. So we dressed up and went out. Ben drove us to the school. He had wanted to take Mom and have all of us go together, but Mom talked him out of it. This was the first time Peter would be back in school for a year and she thought it would be better if he went unchaperoned (except by me).

Of course, with Peter in a wheelchair, we got noticed immediately. I was given an aisle seat, and Peter sat next to me, in the aisle.

"I hope there are no fires," I whispered to him.

"Are you kidding?" he whispered back. "Hop onto my lap, and I'll wheel us both to safety."

"What a comforting thought," I said. "Just don't get trampled to death during intermission."

The play began and I sat back and enjoyed it. Anna was really very good. She was definitely an amateur in a high school production, but she'd learned enough from me to look a lot slicker than everybody else, and she had enough talent to make Antigone come alive. I was very proud of her.

"What do you think?" I asked Peter when intermission began.

"You would have been better," he said.

"That's not what I was asking," I said.

"She is good," he conceded.

"Peter. Hey, Pete."

I turned around. Standing behind Peter were three kids I vaguely knew who were seniors.

"Rick," Peter said. "And Betsy and Dave. This is great. What are you guys doing here?"

"Slumming," Rick said. "What are you doing here? And how are you?"

"Are you coming back to school?" Betsy asked.

"No, not yet," Peter said. "Do you know Leigh?"

"Everybody knows Leigh," Betsy said. I wasn't sure I liked the way she said it.

"Leigh's my stepsister," Peter said. "And a lot of her friends are in the show, so we decided to see it together."

"It's great to see you," Rick said. "You must be feeling a lot better if you're getting out."

"Strong like bull," Peter said.

"That's great," Rick said. "Look, Peter, we've got to get together sometime soon. Play a little chess maybe."

"I'd like that," Peter said.

"We have to get going now," Dave said. "It was good seeing you, Peter."

"Sure," Peter said. "Good seeing you too."

"Right," Rick said. "Take care, Peter."

"You too," Peter said ruefully and watched as they walked away.

"Rick seemed very nice," I said to him when they were past hearing distance.

"He was a friend of mine," Peter said. "He used to come over and visit."

"Why doesn't he anymore?" I asked.

"Because it's a drag visiting people who are sick," he said. "And he has better things to do."

"Maybe now that he sees you're better he'll come visit again," I said.

"Maybe," Peter said. "But I wouldn't hold my breath."

The lights dimmed, so I didn't have a chance to scold him. Soon I was engrossed in the play and forgot about Peter altogether.

When the play ended I asked him if it would be all right if I went backstage and congratulated everybody, Anna especially. She had gotten four curtain calls and somebody had sent her a bouquet of roses.

"Sure, go on ahead," Peter said. "I'll be fine here."

"I'll keep him company," Betsy said. She had walked up to Peter and had her hand on his shoulder.

I wasn't that thrilled about leaving Peter in her clutches but I didn't have any choice in the matter. "I'll be back in a few minutes," I said.

"I'll meet you in the lobby," Peter said. "And I'll call Dad and tell him to come pick us up."

"Okay," I said, and after scowling at Betsy's hand, I went backstage. Everything there was chaotic, and very crowded, but I made my way to Anna and kissed her on her cheek.

"You were fantastic," I said.

"I was, wasn't I," she said. "Leigh, I want you to meet my parents. Mom, Dad, this is Leigh Thorpe, the friend I've told you so much about."

"Oh, Leigh," Mrs. Lessing said and grabbed my hand. "It's so wonderful to meet you at last."

"We can't thank you enough," Mr. Lessing said. "The change that's come over Anna—"

"Yes," I said, deciding to cut the conversation off quickly before it got to be too awful for Anna. "Yes, I really was a help with Anna's performance. But her talent made all the difference. Anna is a very good actress."

"We're very proud of her," Mrs. Lessing said. "And so grateful—"

"I really have to say hello to some other people," I said. "Anna, you were great."

"Thanks, Leigh," she said.

I edged my way over to Cathy. She was standing with Andy and about ten other kids.

"Wasn't Anna great?" Cathy said. "She ought to be a professional, don't you think?"

"She was great," I said. "And so were you. You too, Andy."

"You were a big help," Cathy said.

"I couldn't have done it without you," Andy said. Boy, were his eyes blue. Just like Barry's. We made eye contact and I could feel myself melting.

"Really?" I managed to say.

"Really," he said. "Look, we're having a party tonight, just a spur-of-the-moment thing. Please come."

"I'd love to," I said. "Oh damn. I can't. I came with Peter and we really ought to be getting back."

"Oh," Andy said.

"Some other time," I said.

"Sure," he said. "Next year's opening night, maybe."

"Next year," I said. Next lifetime, I thought, kicking myself.

"Did Peter have a good time?" Cathy said.

"Too good," I said, thinking about Betsy's hand. "And I really ought to be getting back to him. I just wanted to tell you all how good you were."

"Thanks," Cathy said. "That means a lot coming from you."

"Really, Andy," I said. "Some other time."

"Really," he said.

I worked my way through the crowds and then ran through the auditorium to the lobby. Peter was in his wheelchair, all alone.

"Dad will be here in a few minutes," he said when he saw me.

"Where's Betsy?" I asked him.

"She had to join the others," he said.

"And she left you here, all by yourself?" I asked indignantly.

"I told her to," Peter said. "I knew you'd be back in a minute."

"Yeah," I said, wishing I was at the party with Andy. "And I knew you'd be here waiting for me."

The funny thing was that as soon as I saw *Antigone* I found I missed acting. Much as I enjoyed Anna's performance and took pride in it, I found myself wondering how I would have done it differently.

Of course when I thought about it seriously, in those dark moments before falling asleep, I knew I really didn't want to go back to the drudgery I'd just escaped from. Granted there was an occasional *Kampbell Kids* script where I was featured, and those had been fun, but for the most part I just had to screech, "Mom, he's teasing me again!"

and that was that. Scripts like *Mary's Story* didn't come along every day. I'd been lucky to get that role; there was no guarantee I'd ever be offered another one that good.

Besides, I reminded myself, I liked my life the way it was. I still got a kick going to a real school with real teachers and real students. I liked being part of a crowd. I liked having kids come over after school; I liked the phone calls. And even if I wasn't dating, there was always Peter to talk to, Peter to enjoy.

Really, I told myself, if I added up all the pluses and all the minuses in my life, there were a lot more pluses. And the minuses that there were might be changed at any moment. After all Andy had asked me out once, he might always do it again. I was living the life I'd fantasized about for more years than I could remember. I had a real family, real friends. My time was my own. I was no longer a freak, outside looking in. And if I missed acting, well, that was to be expected. You can't give up something you've been doing forever and not expect to miss it occasionally.

So there I was, optimistic that total adjustment was just around the corner, when Barry Cooper called.

"Barry!" I cried, delighted to hear his voice. "Where are you?"

"In New York," he said. "I'm in town for meetings with some producers, so before I left L.A. I called your agent and got your number. How are you, kid?"

"I'm fine," I said. "Oh, I'd love to see you."

"Why do you think I called?" he said. "What do you want to do? Come into the city and start the rumor mongers going? I bet it's been awhile since you've been in a gossip column."

I'd never been in a gossip column, except once when I had my tonsils removed, and he knew it. "You could come out here," I said. "Experience Americana firsthand. And have a home-cooked meal. I bet you're still much too skinny."

"Slender," he said. "Lean. Never skinny. Does your mother still make that great lasagna?"

"Are you kidding?" I said. "She's a housewife now. She does nothing but cook and clean all day."

"Great," Barry said. "Maybe not for her, but it sounds wonderful to me. I'm free tomorrow night."

That's what I'd always liked about Barry, his directness. "Fine," I said, seeing no reason why it shouldn't be. I gave him directions for getting here from the city and we hung up.

Mom didn't mind the unexpected dinner guest (she'd always had a soft spot in her heart for Barry) and she promptly set out to make a clean house already cleaner. If it's possible to be a stage mother to a house, my mother was.

I went to Peter's room, where he was playing the guitar. Finally, he glanced up.

"Company tomorrow night," I announced, feeling a little giddy about it. "Barry Cooper."

"That has-been?" Peter asked, but he grinned. "He's coming out here to see you? That's great."

"He's in New York anyway," I said.

"Even so," Peter said. "A lot of people manage to skip Long Island on their New York City trips."

"That's true enough," I said. "Mom's going to make lasagna, which is Barry's favorite. Maybe he's been in touch with everybody. I'd love to know what they're all up to."

"You miss all that, don't you?" Peter said.

"A little," I admitted. "I'm really enjoying myself but I was a Kampbell Kid for four years. I kind of got used to it. And even if I didn't like some of the people I worked with, I'd still like to know how they're doing."

"Then it'll be good for you to have someone to reminisce with," Peter said. "Although please try to keep your anecdotes to under four hours. I bore easily."

Peter was the least bored person I'd ever met, which always impressed me about him. I'd go crazy stuck in a bed or wheelchair all the time, but he always managed to entertain himself. He was currently hanging out in the kitchen with Mom, learning how to cook.

"I've got to call Cathy and tell her," I said. "She loves Barry."

"Wait a second," Peter said. "Is that wise?"

"What?" I said, thinking he meant was it wise for Cathy to love Barry.

"She doesn't really love Barry," Peter said. "She loves Barry playing Chuck Kampbell."

"True," I said.

"So it probably isn't too wise to invite her over for dinner," he continued. "Besides, if you invite Cathy, the other girls will be jealous."

"Cathy's one of my two best friends," I said weakly. What I was realizing was that I didn't want to invite Cathy over. It wasn't an evening for Leigh Thorpe, suburban kid. It was one for Leigh Thorpe, pro. "I never planned on inviting her," I said. "Just telling her."

"Then she'll be jealous," Peter said. "And resentful. You want to cope with that?"

"But it's not fair not to tell her," I said.

"It's fairer than telling her and then not letting her meet him," Peter said.

He was right. "Okay," I said, starting to feel sorry I wasn't going to be able to show off. "I'll keep my mouth shut."

"That'll be the day," Peter said. I would have kicked him except for his condition, so I just scowled and left the room.

As I expected, school the next day was nerve-wracking. Every time I started to say something I stopped, to make sure I wasn't going to be leaking any secrets. It was very unsettling. When I got home I took a quick look at the homework I knew I wasn't going to get done, then took a shower, put on makeup, and dressed for dinner. I'd offered my services to Mom beforehand but she and Peter were busy making radish roses and told me to keep out of the kitchen, so I did gladly.

Ben came home to find me setting the table with linen napkins and the best silver. Mom was bathing and Peter had been promoted from radishes to carrot curls.

"Everybody's crazy," Ben said, then pitched in by selecting two excellent bottles of wine.

Barry was due at seven thirty and he arrived promptly. He was greeted by a house that could have come straight out of *House Beautiful* and a family that, except for Peter in his wheelchair, could have posed for a postage stamp of great American families.

I broke the pose by running up to Barry and kissing him. It was so good to see him. I'd known it would be, but I hadn't expected to be quite that happy. We hugged, then he hugged my mother. "How are you, Angie?" he asked. "You look fantastic."

"I'm fine," she said. "I'd like you to meet my husband, Ben Sanders, and my stepson, Peter."

Everybody shook hands. Ben offered Barry a drink but he said he'd wait until dinner. Barry then took me by the hand, swung me around, and we embraced again.

"Leigh, you look fantastic," he said. "So grown-up without that braid."

"Thank you," I said. "So tell me, what are you in town for?"

"It's too soon to say for sure," Barry said, and we started making our way into the dining room. "But there's a chance I'll be starring in a Broadway show next year."

"That would be great!" I said. "Do you have the voice for it?"

Barry laughed. "That's what I always liked about you," he said. "The way you come straight to the point. We're not sure, actually, so I'm going to be taking voice lessons for a while, to learn to project better."

"They amplify voices anyway," Peter said.

"That's true," Barry said. "But I've got to be as

close to perfect as possible. There's going to be a lot of people out to get me, reviewers and columnists, because I'm just one of those TV idols. How can I possibly act or sing? Let alone on precious Broadway."

"Then why bother doing it?" Peter asked.

Barry grinned. I melted all over again. "First of all, it's a great property," he said. "And secondly, it's something I want to prove to everybody else and myself that I'm capable of doing."

"Sometimes you have to try for something you might fail at," Ben said. "That's what life's all about."

I hoped Barry wouldn't find Ben's platitudes silly, but if he did, he didn't say so. Instead he said, "That's it exactly. I'd rather try and fail. Besides, if I succeed it just may save my career."

"Barry, you must have gotten lots of offers after *The Kampbell Kids*," Mom said. She was carrying in the antipasto, which she put down and joined us at the table.

"This looks great," Barry said. "Sure I got offers, but nothing I could take seriously. A porno flick. Another series playing the exact same character under a different name. I'm twenty-six years old and I look like I'm eighteen and that makes it tricky to be respected."

"The awkward age," I said.

Barry smiled at me. "Sort of," he said. "Although that seems to be an age you skipped entirely."

"Me?" I said, remembering years of makeup over pimples and at least one anxiety-ridden debate between my mother and a producer over training bras.

"I saw that TV movie you did," Barry said. "You were incredible. I always knew you were good, but I'd never realized you had that kind of range. I envy you."

"Thank you," I said, trying not to burst. That was just the kind of praise I'd been hoping to hear after the movie was on.

"We were very pleased with Leigh's performance," Mom said. "Although it did cause her a certain amount of trouble in school."

"Why?" Barry asked and soon we were all of us telling him different stories about my first few months at school.

We were having a fine time eating lasagna and telling different high school horror stories when the phone rang. I got it.

"Hello," I said, still chuckling over one of Ben's stories.

"Hi," Cathy said. "What's so funny?"

"Nothing," I said. "We were all just sitting around talking."

"Are you busy?" she asked.

"Kind of," I said, at which point Barry started telling a story.

"Who's that?" Cathy asked.

I almost said Peter, but it so obviously wasn't, there was no point saying so. "It's a friend of Ben's," I said instead.

"He sounds familiar," Cathy said.

At which point Barry concluded his story and burst out laughing. Barry's voice isn't all that distinctive, but you can't miss his laugh.

"That sounds just like Barry Cooper," Cathy said.

"He does a little," I said, starting to feel desperate.

"It couldn't be," Cathy said, "could it?"

"Don't be silly," I said. "What would he be doing here?"

"He knows you," she said. "It's possible, isn't it?"

"I met the President once too," I said. "But he doesn't exactly drop by."

"I never knew you met the President," Cathy said.

"It's a long story," I said. "Look, I really want to get back. Why'd you call?"

"Just to talk," she said.

Barry laughed again, this time at something Peter said. I could have killed.

"Are you sure?" she said.

"Positive," I said. "I'll see you tomorrow."

"If I find out that Barry Cooper was at your house and you didn't tell me, then I promise I'll kill you," Cathy said. "Tear you limb from limb."

"I promise you won't find out," I said. "I mean, it would be hard to find that out if it isn't so."

"All right," Cathy said, although she still sounded downright suspicious. "I'll see you tomorrow."

"Bye," I said, and hung up quickly before Barry found anything more to laugh at. I went back to the table and raised my eyebrows at Peter, who knew exactly who had called. But I was damned if I was going to worry about Cathy and her suspicions and instead relaxed and stayed up until past midnight reminiscing and catching up on gossip with Barry.

Finally we all realized how late it was—and Barry had a long drive back. I put on my coat and walked him out to his car. We stood for a moment in the cold, clear December night and looked first at the stars and then at each other.

"So how's it going, kid?" Barry asked. "Really?"

"All right," I said, feeling a lot like Chris Kampbell talking to her big brother. "Some of it I really like, like not having to memorize scripts.

And some of it I miss. The shop talk. The sense of being someone special."

"That's the hardest to give up," Barry said. "Lots of people can't."

"I think I can," I said. "I like being normal. I like having friends and going to football games."

"You got cheated out of all that," Barry said. "Not that I can remember high school as anything great."

"Nobody'll date me," I said. "I never get asked out."

"What about Peter?" Barry asked.

"Peter doesn't date," I said. "Besides, he doesn't count."

"No captains of the football team?" Barry asked sympathetically. "No class presidents?"

"No water boys!" I wailed.

"They're probably still intimidated," he said. "That may not improve until you go to college."

"But that's almost two years away," I said.

"Maybe it won't take that long," he said. "Maybe some really daring boy'll ask you out, and after the first one does you'll probably get more dates. But give it time. They're scared of you. They'd be scared just because you're so pretty, but since you're an actress it makes you scarier."

"I might as well just get a pair of fangs," I said. "The Werewolf of Long Island."

Barry laughed. "I have to get going," he said. "Keep me posted on developments."

"I will," I promised, and we kissed good-bye.

Cathy didn't say anything to me the next day about dinner guests, which was just as well since I was tired and giddy and might have blown the whole thing. The following day, though, she came in at lunchtime and said, "Barry Cooper was in New York this week."

"Really?" I said.

"Really," she said. "It was in yesterday's paper. Just twenty miles away from here."

"What are you talking about?" Andy asked. "I have the feeling I walked into the middle of something."

"Just that I have this feeling that Barry Cooper was over at Leigh's house the other night," Cathy said. "And Leigh doesn't want us peasants to know it."

"I've never thought of myself as a peasant," Anna said. "Who's Barry Cooper?"

Cathy ignored her. "Are you going to keep on denying it?" she asked me.

"Sure," I said. "I'll keep on denying it."

"Barry Cooper was over at your house?" Andy said. "Did he just drop in or did you have a date or what?"

"Yeah, what?" Sharon asked. "I loved Barry Cooper for years."

"Who's Barry Cooper?" Anna asked Bob.

"Just a teen-age idol," he replied.

"Just a teen-age idol," Cathy said. "The teen-age idol of my dreams. Right in this very town, at my dear friend's house, and does she tell me? No. What's the matter, afraid I'd shame you?"

"Honestly, Cathy," I said, but I didn't feel quite right saying that. The last thing I intended to be was honest.

"Did you date him in Hollywood?" Andy asked.

"No, of course not," I said.

"But he liked you," Cathy said. "You admitted that to me. So if he was in town naturally he'd drop by to say hello."

"You would be astounded at the number of people I know who come to New York and don't drop by to see me," I said. "Now, can we change the subject?"

"All right," Cathy said. "Don't you think, everybody, that trust is the basis of every real friendship?"

"Oh, good grief," I muttered. Where was Peter when I needed him? Leading a double life could be awfully tricky, especially if your only ally was home, unable to help.

Chapter
8

I'd spoken to my father a few times since I'd moved back east, but except for one quick lunch we hadn't seen each other. In early December we made plans for me to spend a weekend with him. I was really looking forward to it. I spent Friday night at home, but Saturday morning I took the train into New York and my father met me at the station.

"You didn't have to," I told him after we hugged. "I could have found your place."

"I know," he said. "But I liked the image of meeting you here."

So I let him take my bag. We walked outside and Dad hailed a cab. He gave the cabby his West Seventy-ninth Street address. It was a nice ride.

"There's someone I'd like you to meet," Dad said after tipping the driver and grabbing my suitcase. "A wonderful woman."

"Anything serious?" I asked. Dad had remarried once after Mom, but it hadn't worked out. Since then he'd sworn never to get married again. My father's oaths are notoriously short-lived however.

"Serious enough," he admitted as we got into the elevator. "We've been living together for a few months now."

"That's great," I said. "Going to get married?"

"Never," Dad said. "Lynn doesn't want to get married either. She's twice burnt too."

"What does she do?" I asked.

"She acts," he said.

I gave him a look.

"I don't have anything to say to other people," he said. "I might as well stick with actresses."

"There's a whole world out there," I said. "Full of interesting secretaries and dentists."

"I am fatally attracted to actresses," he said. "But Lynn's someone special. She's dying to meet you."

We got out of the elevator and Dad unlocked his apartment door.

It was a good-looking apartment, high white walls, with a stained glass window in the enormous living room. "This is really nice, Dad," I said. I wasn't surprised though. Dad always lives well.

"God bless Lefty O'Roarke," he said. "He's keeping me in clover. Honey, we're here."

"Be right there," a voice said, coming out of what I assumed was the bedroom. I felt vaguely nervous and was relieved when a nice-looking woman of about thirty-five came out. Dad's taste frequently ran to younger women.

"Hi, Leigh," she said. "I'm Lynn Marsh."

"Hi, Lynn," I said.

"Sit down," Dad said. "Leigh, would you like something to eat or drink? Coffee?"

"No thanks," I said, taking a seat. "I ate breakfast before I left."

"How's your mother?" Dad asked.

"She's fine," I said. "She seems to have adjusted to being a housewife very easily."

"That's good," he said. "Of course she must be busy taking care of Peter."

"She doesn't mind," I said. "We all like Peter a lot."

"Good," he said. "Lynn has a son too."

"Yes?" I said and involuntarily looked around for a kid.

"He lives with his father," Lynn said. "More stability."

"Oh," I said. "How did you and Dad meet?"

"Lynn's on *Joys and Sorrows* too," Dad said.

"Oh that's right," I said. "I knew you looked familiar. You're Alice."

Lynn smiled. "You watch the show?"

"When I'm home," I said. "Mostly to see Dad. The two of you don't have many scenes together."

"I think we've only done one," Dad said. "But we'd meet at rehearsals and go out for drinks afterward and we discovered we liked each other."

"He was so menacing," Lynn said. "On camera at least. And off he was no nice. I wanted to get to know him better."

"That's great," I said. "Who's apartment is this?"

Lynn laughed. "It's your father's," she said. "I moved out of my little hovel about three months ago."

"We're very happy," Dad said.

"Why don't I show Leigh her room?" Lynn said. "This apartment, bless it, has four rooms, so there's space for overnight guests. Here," she said as I followed her down a hallway. "The couch turns into a bed at night. It's pretty comfortable, I'm told."

"This is very nice," I said. They used the extra room as a den. There were books and records and a wall of photographs and clippings about Dad and Lynn as well as a few about me.

"I saw that TV movie you made," Lynn said. "Your performance was remarkable. Your father was so proud of you."

"Thank you," I said. "It seems like ages since I made it."

"You haven't worked since?" she asked.

"Voluntary retirement," I said.

"I'd go crazy," she said. "I once went for six months without being able to get a job and I was climbing the walls."

"What about when you were pregnant?" I asked.

"I worked all through it," she said. "I was Donna on *Never Look Back* then and she was forever getting pregnant. Nobody noticed one more."

"I worked on *Tomorrow's Destiny* for a while," I said. "Years ago."

"I know," Lynn said. "Your father's told me all about your career. He's very proud of you."

"I'm proud of him too," I said.

"That means a lot to him," she said. "But enough of this serious talk. Your father has a full day planned for you and I think he'll be heartbroken if you miss a single thing."

"I'll be suicidal," Dad called, so we joined him and I listened to the itinerary.

First we went out for lunch and then the three

of us went to a matinee. The show had three major teen-age parts and I knew one of the actresses from a guest spot she'd done on *The Kampbell Kids*, so we went backstage after the show and I chatted briefly with her. It had been so long since I'd been in a play, I asked her what the routine was like.

"Hectic but structured," she said. "I'll be graduating from high school this June and that'll make things easier."

I told her about having seen Barry, but it turned out he'd seen the same musical and had gone backstage to say hello too.

"Our dinner reservation isn't for a while," Dad said. "So I thought maybe you'd enjoy going to a museum?"

"That sounds fine," I said. Lynn bowed out, saying she was tired and wanted to take a little nap before supper, so we agreed we'd meet her back at the apartment. I realized it was possible she was giving Dad and me some time alone. I gave her a couple of points for that.

"L.A. was all right," Dad said as we walked through the Museum of Modern Art. "But I missed the museums and the theaters and the cultural life New York has to offer."

"You're going to stay here awhile?" I asked.

"For as long as they need Lefty O'Roarke," he

said. "Of course, with villains you never know. No job security."

"But you're such a good villain," I said. "They'll hold on to you for a long time."

"I hope so," Dad said as we stood in front of a Matisse. "They can't reform me. Who ever heard of a hero named Lefty? So it's just a matter of time. I think I'm going to get murdered pretty soon."

"That's terrible," I said. "But you should be able to get another job pretty quickly."

Dad laughed. "Want to put that in writing?" he asked.

Dinner was really nice. We had it in a good restaurant with friends of Dad and Lynn, a married couple with a seventeen-year-old daughter. The husband was a TV writer and his wife a soap opera actress, so their daughter was used to show business people and wasn't the least bit shy with me.

The next day, after a New York City brunch of lox and bagels, Dad and I went to Queens and saw the Jets play the L.A. Rams. Dad explained that he had season tickets and usually went with Lynn. She got some more points. The Rams slaughtered the Jets, but I was ambivalent about who to root for anyway, so I didn't mind. It was a perfect football day, not too cold and very sunny. I had a fine time.

"I don't want to go home," I said on the subway going back. "Not yet."

"Stay an extra day," Dad said. "Call your mother and see if it's okay with her. I'm working tomorrow, but I'd love to take you to the set."

So I called Mom, who said if I wouldn't be missing anything too important at school I could stay. I didn't have any tests scheduled, and rarely missed school, so we decided it was a safe day for me to cut.

Lynn had to work that day too, so we all got up early, dressed, and went down to the studio. I'd worked at a different network for *Tomorrow's Destiny* but it didn't matter; it felt like coming home. Just seeing the lights and cameras gave me a happy rush.

There was a line rehearsal first, and then the actors and director blocked the scene. I stayed on the sidelines, watching as they worked. Dad was very good. He menaced with the best of them. But he was right. I could tell from undercurrents in the script that his character wasn't long for this world. Three different characters offered reasons why they wished Lefty O'Roarke was dead. I gave him another two months at the most. Poor Dad. There went his job stability, his season tickets. If he didn't look so evil, he might get a job as a hero and work for years and years on the same show, but there was something shifty about his eyes that kept him from sympathetic parts. Maybe he'd get into a long-running Broadway show, or maybe another soap would need a resident villain in the immediate future. Otherwise, it was months on the unemployment line and constant auditions. I'd never been that route, but I knew enough actors, my father included, to know what it was like.

There was a long lunch break before shooting, and as soon as rehearsal broke up Dad came over with one of the actors.

"Leigh, this is Garry Murdoch," he said. "Garry, my daughter Leigh."

"I know Leigh," Garry said. "Although she may not remember it, since it was years ago. I was her father on *Tomorrow's Destiny*."

"You were?" I asked. "This is awful, but I don't remember working with you."

"I couldn't acknowledge you, so we didn't have many scenes together," Garry said. "Mostly I looked at you from afar and wished I could tell the world."

"Did you ever get a chance to?"

"Yeah, but by then you were eighteen and pregnant," he said.

125

"Hey," Dad said. "That's funny. Here's Leigh with her two fathers and they're both working on the same show."

"That is cute," Garry said. "Maybe we should tell the publicity department."

"I think so," Dad said. "You don't mind, do you, honey?"

I did, but I certainly wasn't going to say so. Before I knew it, there was a photographer snapping pictures of the three of us.

"They'll send the pictures to the different soap fan magazines," Garry said. "Painless publicity."

Painless for them. For me it probably meant another lecture from Peter. Still, there were things you had to do for your father. And it had been so long since I'd had my picture taken, I almost missed it. So I smiled while the photographer snapped.

They let me watch from the control booth while they were shooting. I admit I got a little jealous watching the actors act. Memorizing lines isn't fun, but acting sure is. There's a real joy in pretending to be somebody else, in knowing what you're doing and knowing you're doing it well.

Dad and Lynn took me back to the train station and I kissed them both good-bye. I'd gotten rather fond of Lynn and the way she disparaged the nice things she did. "I hate football," she'd told me after I thanked her for the use of her ticket. "I only go because your father likes to so much."

I gave Dad a big hug and we agreed we had to do this again very soon. I appreciated all the effort he'd gone to for the weekend and I wanted him to know it.

"I'm just glad to have a chance to see you," he said. "It's silly, your just being out on the Island and us acting like you're still on the coast. We have to get together more regularly."

"We will," I promised and got on the train. Something Garry had said had me thinking.

He'd asked me if I'd gotten many job offers after my TV movie and I'd told him that I hadn't gotten any.

"That's funny," he said. "You were so good I'd have thought your agent would have been flooded with calls."

I realized as I sat on the train that I didn't know for sure that I hadn't gotten any calls. I'd just assumed I hadn't since my agent hadn't called me to say. So as soon as I got home, I decided, I'd give her a call and find out. Just for curiosity's sake, since I obviously wasn't about to take any jobs. But it would be nice to know I'd gotten some offers.

Mom hadn't known what train I'd be making, so I took a cab home from the train station. When I got there she was out buying groceries and Peter was alone.

I gave him a quick kiss and told him I had to make a phone call. He looked at me quizzically but didn't say anything as I dialed my agent's number. It felt funny calling it after all those months.

I was placed through as soon as I told her secretary who it was and how I'd been. In a moment there was Betty, sounding as though she were right next door and not three thousand miles away.

"Leigh, darling," she said. "It's so great to hear from you. How are you?"

So I told her I was fine and what I'd been up to. "Betty," I said, after we'd exchanged some more small talk, "I was wondering about something."

"What, dear?" she asked.

"I didn't expect people to be tearing my walls down, but I did think somebody might have offered me a job since *The Kampbell Kids*," I said nervously. What if nobody had?

"Of course there have been offers," Betty said. "Why, dear, are you thinking about coming back?"

"No, of course not," I said. "But there have been offers?"

"Certainly," she said. "I've told your mother about the ones I thought she should know about."

"I see," I said. "Mom knows about them then?"

"Of course," Betty said. "And how is your mother?"

So we talked about her and Dad for a while, and then as soon as I could I hung up. "Interesting," I said to no one in particular.

"What?" Peter asked.

"Nothing," I said. "Just something I have to talk to Mom about."

Mom cooperated by coming in a couple of minutes later. I helped her with the groceries and as we unpacked them I told her about the call.

"What kind of offers?" I asked, putting the vegetables away.

"What difference does it make?" Mom said. "You can't take them."

"I'd still like to know," I said.

"All right," Mom said. "There were only four that Betty thought were worth my attention, so there were probably more she didn't bother telling me about."

"Four?" I said, starting to feel a little more important. "What were they?"

"One was a commercial," Mom said. "I certainly couldn't see you flying out just for a commercial. The second was to play a new character on *A Doctor's Life*."

"Wait a second," I said. "That sounds good. What kind of character?"

"Dr. Henderson's daughter," Mom said. "You would have been in six episodes. They cast somebody else instead."

"Damn," I said. "What else did you decide wasn't worth my time?"

"There was a pilot for a comedy show," Mom said. "You would have been playing Chris under a different name. And there was another TV movie."

"What was the movie about?"

"It didn't sound very good," Mom said. "You would have gotten fourth billing and your part wasn't very big."

"And you turned all this stuff down without consulting me?" I asked.

"I consulted you," Mom said. "Last summer I said, 'Do you want to keep on here while I move east, or do you want to come with me?' And you said you wanted to come with me and be a normal American teen-ager. I think those were your exact words. And I believed you. Was I wrong to?"

"No, of course not," I said. "It's just . . . why couldn't I have done the pilot at least?"

"Because what if the network bought it?" Mom asked. "Then you'd be stuck in the same routine you complained about for four years."

"Dr. Henderson's daughter," I said. "That sounds meaty."

"I'll tell you the truth," Mom said. "The way Betty explained it to me, it wasn't meaty at all. It was comic relief. You were supposed to have a cute little crush on Dr. Wilson and you'd pop up once a month and sigh over him. You would have been needed there maybe one week a month, but it would have totally disrupted any schedule we would have set up. It just didn't sound worth it."

"I hate Dr. Wilson," I said. "He's the one that always gets the girls, right?"

"They always die," Mom said. "Worthless doctor."

I laughed. "I guess I'm stuck here for a while then," I said.

"Is that the way you feel about it?" Mom asked. "Stuck?"

"No," I said. "I think it was just seeing Dad's show and all. It gave me itchy feet. I'll calm down again."

"I hope so," Mom said. "Because this is my life now. We could make other arrangements for you if you really wanted, but I had hoped you'd stay here until you graduated high school."

"I'm going to," I said. "You're right. I complained all the time when I worked. I've just forgotten how lousy it was, that's all."

"Do you want me to tell you about any other offers you might get?" Mom asked.

"Yeah, please," I said quickly. "I won't take them, but I would like to know."

"I would have told you before if I'd thought you were interested," she said.

"I know," I said. "It's okay. That part of my life is over with. I like what I have now." I gave her a kiss and walked out to the living room. Peter was sitting there, watching, appropriately enough, a rerun of *The Kampbell Kids*.

"You're going to be stuck with me for quite a while longer," I said to him as I watched an image of myself three years younger on the screen.

"Stuck?" Peter said. "I don't feel stuck."

"Neither do I," I said. "I guess."

Chapter
9

As the fall turned into winter, it was obvious there was a change in Peter. Mom, Ben, and I didn't talk about it much, but we all noticed it and were pleased by it.

For one thing, his physical condition improved. Partly that was just the nature of the disease— some times were better than others—but a lot of it was due to Peter's newfound devotion to his physical therapy. Before, it had been an effort to get him to go to his physical therapy sessions; now he was eager to go and continued to exercise when he got home. In fact, his doctor was a little concerned that Peter might be overdoing it. On his better days Peter was out of his wheelchair and using crutches to get around. Ben was worried that Peter might slip on an ice patch, so Peter used his wheelchair outside. In spite of the problems of maneuvering it, he insisted that we go Christmas shopping together. Mom chauffeured us to the nearest shopping mall, but we left her at a clothes shop as we made our way through a half dozen other shops while Peter searched for presents for her, Ben, his mother, and Jim, his tutor. Things got a little tricky in the Christmas crowds, and entirely too many people stared at Peter or whispered "poor boy" within hearing distance, but except for occasionally asking strangers if they'd care to see a wheelie, Peter ignored it all.

We had one fine Christmas too. I liked the snow and the need for a whole new wardrobe and the way Christmas lights looked on houses without palm trees in their yards. And there was something nice about celebrating Christmas in December; for the past four years we'd taped our Christmas show sometime in October, complete with fake snow. The real thing at the real time was rather pleasant.

Ben, Mom, and I put the Christmas tree up and decorated it with great care while Peter coached us and helped with the decorations on the lower branches. Peter was all for stringing popcorn and cranberries, doing a real hokey job, but the rest of us wouldn't go quite that far. Still, the tree looked very American; I was a little sorry there were no fan magazines to take pictures of it.

We exchanged our presents—Peter gave me the cast album from my favorite Broadway show and I gave him a brand-new, very technical book about chess that scared me just to look at. Then we ate a perfectly enormous dinner. The next day I went into New York and spent four days at Dad's place, visiting with him and running around the city. By the time I got back all I could think about was exams and papers, so I spent the rest of the vacation catching up on school work. Sharon gave a New Year's Eve party, but Mom and Ben had been invited to a party and I didn't want to leave Peter alone. Besides, I didn't have a date and I didn't want to go to it alone. So Peter and I toasted the New York by ourselves. Peter seemed very optimistic that night.

"The worst is over," he assured me. "For both of us. From here on in, things are going to go fine."

Right after New Year's, Ben went away on a business trip, the kind he used to take while he was courting Mom. Three days in Chicago, a week in L.A. I had the feeling Mom wished she could be going with him, but she decided to stay with Peter and me instead.

I wouldn't have minded going myself; by then I was bored with East Coast weather. I'd forgotten in the years I'd lived in California just how cold and yucky it can get in January.

About a week after Ben left, Peter came down with the flu. Mom called Dr. Loeb, who came over, checked him out, and recommended bed rest, fluids, and antibiotics. Peter sighed and sniffled and made Mom's and my life miserable with constant demands for company, soup, and tissues.

"This is what I gave up stardom for?" I asked rhetorically.

Actually, when Peter was sleeping it was nice being alone with Mom again. We couldn't leave the house at the same time, so a lot of times when I was home from school, she'd use the chance to do some shopping while I baby-sat. But late at night we stayed up talking the way we used to before Ben and Peter entered our lives. It was nice being alone with Mom again. I liked Ben and I loved Peter, but I enjoyed those times anyway.

Everything got shot to hell when Ben came home. Naturally, after kissing Mom and saying hello to me, he asked after Peter.

"Peter's in bed," Mom said.

"Why? What's the matter?"

"Nothing," she said. "He has the flu."

"The flu?" Ben asked and went into Peter's room to check for himself. We followed him in. "Peter, are you all right?"

Peter had spent the past three days complaining. Fortunately he came through for us. "I'm fine, Dad," he said. "Just a bad cold."

"Angie says it's the flu," Ben said, going to Peter's bedside and checking Peter's forehead with his hand.

"So it's the flu," Peter said and sneezed.

"Has Dr. Loeb seen you?" Ben asked.

"Of course," Peter said. "I sneezed twice and Angie sent for him." He sneezed twice as though to demonstrate. I wished Dr. Loeb would materialize.

"I'm going to call him," Ben said.

"Ben, that's hardly necessary," Mom said. "He gave me a prescription, and Peter's been taking his medication regularly. Dr. Loeb really didn't seem that concerned."

"He probably didn't want to alarm you," Ben said, looking worriedly at Peter. Peter looked disgusted.

"Dad, I'm not dying of pneumonia," he said. "Look, call Dr. Loeb if it'll make you feel any better."

"How long has he been sick?" Ben asked.

"Since Wednesday," Mom said.

"Wednesday!" Ben said. "I called you Thursday and you never said a word about it to me."

"I couldn't see any point," Mom said. "Dr. Loeb had already been here and he'd assured me there was nothing to worry about. But I knew you'd worry."

"Of course I'd worry," Ben said. "This is my son."

"Who happens to have the flu," Mom said. "Honestly, Ben, if Leigh had the flu do you think I'd be carrying on like this?"

"Leigh is not a hemophiliac," Ben said. "Leigh doesn't have a history of upper respiratory diseases. Leigh did not have pneumonia three times before she was twelve."

I stared at Peter with new respect.

"If there had been any kind of emergency, I would have told you," Mom said. "But there wasn't and I knew you would overreact and cut your trip short and come back here where there was nothing you could do except behave like an overprotective mother lion, which is hardly what Peter needs."

"What Peter needs is for you to get out of here," Peter said. "I mean that, Dad. You too, Angie. If you're going to fight about me, you could at least do it someplace where I won't have to listen."

"Peter, I'm sorry," Mom said.

"Angie, please," Peter said wearily. "Let me sneeze in peace."

Mom and Ben looked apologetically at Peter and left the room. I lingered, not sure whether I'd also been dismissed.

"Damn," Peter said when the adults were gone.

"Excuse me?" I said.

"Damn everything," Peter said. "Damn this disease and damn the flu and damn beds and tissues and feeling lousy. Damn my goddamn body."

I moved closer to his bed. "It's okay," I said. "Married people fight. That's part of marriage."

"Where did you pick up that bit of wisdom?" Peter asked savagely. "From *The Kampbell Kids*? Or maybe from *Mary's Story*?"

"I learned it from life," I said. "I have divorced parents too."

Peter was silent for a moment. "Yeah," he said finally. "That's a comfort, I guess."

"What do you mean?" I asked.

"Nothing," he said. "Just that I'm not the cause of all marriages breaking up."

"Oh, Peter," I said. "Mom and Ben aren't splitting up."

"How do you know?" he asked.

"I don't know," I said. "But I don't know that

they *are* splitting up either, so why should I assume they are?"

"If they do split up, it'll be my fault," he said. "It was my fault that Mom and Dad got divorced."

"I don't believe that," I said.

"You weren't here," he said. "The fights, the tensions—they all revolved around me. I was sick so much, and Mom was so guilty about it, she couldn't cope. She never would have gotten involved with Don if I'd been healthy. He was a way for her to escape."

"That doesn't make it your fault," I said. "It's only your fault . . . oh, I don't know. If you put itching powder in their bed, then it's your fault. Just existing doesn't make you responsible."

"Itching powder?"

"I'm upset too," I said. "Look, my parents had a miserable marriage for years before they finally got divorced. Just awful. My mother has an incredible pain threshold when it comes to marriage."

"So?" he asked.

"So by the time she gets sick of Ben's overprotectiveness, which she probably will, you'll be long gone. To college, I mean. Probably married with kids of your own by then, and you just won't be an issue anymore."

"Dad's going to be protective of me until the day I die," Peter said.

"Which will be when you're ninety," I said. "Boring everybody with stories about how much pneumonia you had as a kid."

"That's a nice thought," Peter said. "I'd like to live long enough to be boring."

"I hate to be the one to tell you this, sweetie," I said, "but you've already lived that long. In spades."

Peter sneezed. "No pity for the sick," he said.

"You really want pity?" I asked.

"Not from you," he said. "Go and see if anybody's made plane reservations for Reno."

"Okay," I said. "But don't get your hopes up. I'm afraid you're going to be stuck with Mom and me for quite a while longer."

I left Peter's room, carefully closing the door behind me, and found Mom and Ben in the kitchen.

"Don't say it," Ben said as I came in. "I know I behaved like an idiot. I've already apologized to your mother; now let me apologize to you."

I shrugged my shoulders. "People fight," I said. "But you upset Peter."

"I can imagine," Ben said. "Is he all right now?"

"He's okay," I said.

"I'll go in now and talk to him," Ben said. "Leigh, I really am sorry. The plane was late and we circled over Kennedy for over an hour and it wouldn't have taken much to set me off."

"We all have days like that," I said. Ben smiled at me and left the kitchen.

"Good grief," I said to Mom after he was gone.

"He was very apologetic," Mom said. "Really, just a tempest in a teapot."

"Do me a favor," I said. "Stay married to Ben for a while. Like for the next ten or twenty years. And then if you do get a divorce, make sure it's because Ben's having an affair with a giraffe. For my sake too, but mostly for Peter's."

Everybody else's mood might have improved after that, but mine got worse. I hated the weather and the sameness of everything. School and family, family and school. Nothing exciting ever happened, except Peter's getting sick, and that certainly was no fun. Finally Mom took me aside for one of her earnest mother-daughter conferences.

"What the hell is going on with you?" she asked.

"What do you mean?" I asked.

"I haven't seen you wear anything but jeans in weeks," she said. "You don't have to wear dresses or skirts, not in this weather, but you own some perfectly nice slacks."

"I like jeans," I said.

"You haven't worn makeup in ages," Mom said.

"Not even mascara. And your hair needs cutting and your nails are a mess."

"Mom, I'm not in the business anymore," I said. "I don't have to look good all the time."

"I'm not talking about looking like a model," Mom said. "Just common neatness. And you're grouchy all the time."

"Not all the time," I said. "Just almost all the time."

Mom smiled. "What's the matter, honey?" she asked. "Do you want to talk about it?"

"There's nothing to talk about," I said. "I'm just feeling a little depressed. It's February."

"What can we do to un-depress you?" she asked. "There must be something."

"I don't know," I said.

"How about if we all go out to dinner tonight?" Mom asked. "It would be good for Peter too."

I thought about how people stared at Peter and shuddered. "I don't think eating out is the solution to everything," I said.

"I never said it would cure everything," Mom said. "I'm not a simpleton, Leigh."

"I know," I said. "I'm sorry. Sure, let's eat out. I'd love something expensive and exotic."

So the four of us ate out at a Japanese restaurant. I hated the weather and the stares we got and the inconvenience of dealing with Peter and his wheelchair, but at least I wasn't wearing blue jeans, which gave Mom one less thing to complain about.

Peter hobbled his way to my room two nights later and knocked on the door. I was lying on my bed, thinking about all the work I should have been doing, and told him to come in.

"You're worse than I am," he said as he came in. "Haven't you ever heard of overhead lights?"

"I was conserving energy," I said.

Peter turned the light switch on anyway. "May I sit down?" he asked.

"Sit," I said.

He took the chair by the desk and eased his way into it. He left his crutches by his side.

"When do you think you'll be able to give those things up?" I asked.

"Not for a while," he said. "But they're very pleased with the progress I'm making."

"Great," I said.

"There's a place in California that offers very intensive therapy," he said. "I'd really have to work there, but they accomplish great things, and if I kept exercising afterward, it could do me a lot of good."

"Are you going to go?" I asked.

"I don't know yet," Peter said. "It costs an awful

lot of money and Dad's expenses have increased lately."

"Don't let Mom and me keep you from going," I said.

"I haven't decided yet," he said. "Anyway, that's not why I'm here."

"Why are you here?" I asked. "Disturbing my perfectly good rest."

"You're resting too much," he said. "You're practically hibernating."

"I'm part grizzly," I said.

"You're part something all right," he said. "Anyway, it seems to me you owe me one party and I'm here to collect."

"What are you talking about?"

"I know what you thought," he said. "You thought I'd let you get away with procrastinating forever. Well, I won't. I've been practicing that guitar for months now, and it's about time we made plans."

"You really want a party?" I asked.

"I insist on it," Peter said. "Is a week from Saturday too soon?"

"Yes," I said, sitting up. "We need two weeks at least."

"Okay," he said. "Two weeks from Saturday. How many guests?"

"I don't know," I said. "This is your party."

"It's *our* party," he said. "But I would like to invite some guests of my own."

"Sure," I said. "Who?"

"Jim and his wife," he said. "Sort of mini-chaperones. I talked to Jim about it and he said it was fine with him. And I'd like to ask a couple of the guys I used to be friends with from school. They haven't been exactly beating a path to my door lately, but I figure if they see I'm still among the living it might make them a little friendlier. Rick. Dave maybe. People like that."

"Great," I said. "I'll invite some of my friends. We'll have twelve people. How does that sound?"

"I'd like it bigger," Peter said. "But for a first effort maybe we should keep it small."

"Cathy and Bob and Sharon and Anna," I said. "And Andy, that creep."

"Why is Andy a creep all of a sudden?" Peter asked.

"Because he's dating Jenny Moskowitz," I said. "I guess I'll have to ask her too."

"You mean to say Andy could have dated you and he's dating somebody else instead?" Peter asked. "He must be crazy."

"You are a sweetheart," I said. "I think he preferred me with my braid. I'd like to braid him one."

Peter laughed. "Anyone else you want to ask?"

"Cathy'll have a date," I said. "She always does. And I think Anna might too."

"Anna's dating somebody?" Peter asked.

"I didn't tell you?" I said. "I guess I haven't been talking to you very much lately."

"I've been busy," he said. "And you've been antisocial. Who's the sucker—I mean, who's Anna dating?"

"You mean who's the sucker, and he isn't," I said. "I only met him once, very briefly, but he seems very nice. He's a junior at Columbia and he and Anna met at a poetry reading in the city. It's all very artsy and passionate."

"Artsy I can see," Peter said. "Passionate, on the other hand . . ."

"That should make an interesting mix," I said, ignoring him. "It'll be nice giving a party where everybody doesn't know everybody else."

"I don't suppose you could get Barry Cooper to make a special guest star appearance," Peter said. "Give the evening some class."

"He's back on the coast," I said. "He called me at my father's."

"Yes, I know," Peter said. "He tried here first."

"I'm glad we're staying in touch," I said. "I feel so cut off from everyone I used to know."

"You don't regret it, do you?" he said. "Giving it all up?"

"A little," I said, then looked at Peter. "Not much," I added. "I think I'm just one of those people destined to want what I don't have."

"All I want is a party," Peter said. "And perfect health. And a million dollars. But I'll settle for a party."

"You're on," I said. "Start tuning your guitar."

I extended verbal invitations to everybody and they all said they'd be delighted to come. Maybe it was hearing the pleasure in their voices as they accepted that picked up my spirits, but I started getting involved with party plans. We moved Peter's stereo into the living room and selected our loudest dancing records. We moved the furniture around, so it looked more partyish and less *House and Garden*, and we removed a few of the more expensive breakables. Ben hid the booze.

"I saw *Mary's Story*," he said. "I'm not taking any chances."

In the end he conceded to beer, since, as we pointed out, we'd be drinking it with or without his blessings. He and Mom also agreed that since Jim and his wife, Terry, would be there, there was no need for them. They made plans to spend the evening playing bridge with friends but vowed to be back by midnight.

Mom and I ran around buying potato chips and that kind of thing, and Mom and Peter made a couple of dips. I got my hair cut, bought a long skirt, and Mom gave me an extensive manicure. Peter got a new sport coat and went to the barber. He looked very dapper.

I was nervous the afternoon of the party, doing the last-minute arrangements and worrying about things working out, but as soon as the doorbell rang with the first guests I knew everything would be okay. Mom and Ben greeted everyone as they came in and then left inconspicuously. Although Jim and Terry were in their twenties, they fit right in and started a lengthy conversation with Anna and her boyfriend. My friends knew Peter's from school, and everybody got along well together. Andy came alone, which surprised me, but everyone else we'd invited showed. After a fair amount of coaxing, Peter was convinced to bring out his guitar, and he stunned me with the quality of his playing. Cathy flirted openly with him. I thought she was a little obvious, but Peter didn't seem to mind, and when we put the records on and started dancing, she kept sitting next to him to talk. That left me free to dance, so I did, with Jim and Bob. We made a lot of noise and had a good time.

At one point I found myself alone in the kitchen, making more ice cubes. I guess because it was so cold outside, I had underestimated how much we'd need. I was pouring water into the trays when Andy came in.

"At last we are alone," he said.

"Don't worry," I said. "I'll be leaving in a second."

"No," he said. "I've been waiting for a chance to be alone with you."

"Oh?" I said, putting the trays back in the freezer.

"Yeah," he said. "I've been feeling bad about something for a long time now and I'd like to apologize once and for all."

"Sure," I said. "What?"

"It's the way I reacted to that movie of yours," he said. "I know I behaved badly and I'm sorry."

"Oh," I said. "Yeah, you were a little hard on me."

"I have a cousin who's an alcoholic," he said. "He's nineteen and he's wrecked his life. I'm sensitive about the subject."

"I can see why," I said. "That's awful. The movie must have been really grating for you."

"That doesn't excuse the way I behaved," he said. "Besides, there's more."

I looked at him expectantly.

"This may sound presumptuous of me," he said. "But I've felt this really strong attraction between us since the first day I talked to you. Do you know what I mean?"

"Oh yes," I said.

"But I was scared about asking you out," he said. "There you were, fresh off television. I figured you knew lots of sophisticated guys in Hollywood. I figured you'd laugh at me if I asked you out."

"I wouldn't have done that," I said.

"Yeah, but by the time I figured that out, that awful movie was on and we had that fight," he said. "When I finally decided it was safe to ask you out, I invited you to the cast party for *Antigone* and it turns out you're dating Peter."

"I wasn't dating Peter," I said.

"You said you were," he said. "That's why you couldn't come to the party."

"Peter is my stepbrother," I said. "He's my friend. We don't date."

"Everybody assumes you do," he said. "You're always talking about him."

"I am not," I said. "Am I?"

"It sure seems that way," he said. "Lots of guys wanted to ask you out, but we thought if you were dating Peter you wouldn't be interested. And frankly, none of us was too crazy about stealing you from a cripple."

I hoped Peter was sitting next to the stereo.

This wasn't the kind of conversation I wanted him to overhear.

"Peter and I don't date," I said. "We went to the play together but it wasn't a date. I've wanted you to ask me out for months now. And I'm sorry if my movie bothered you, but there was no way I could have known it would when I made it since I didn't even know you existed."

"You really wanted me to ask you out?" he asked.

"That's not the kind of thing I lie about," I said.

"What are you doing next Friday night?"

"Nothing," I said.

"How about a movie?" he asked.

"That sounds great," I said.

"Yeah," he said. "It does, doesn't it. Okay, let's go to the movies."

"Okay," I said. "I mean, fantastic."

"I mean fantastic too," he said.

We stood there for a moment feeling very pleased with ourselves. "What did I come in here for anyway?" I asked.

"I don't know," Andy said. "But it probably wasn't important."

"Probably not," I said.

"So why don't we go back out and dance?" he said. "I've been wanting to dance with you all night."

I smiled at him. "That sounds wonderful," I said and we walked back to the living room, where we danced five straight dances together.

The party broke up around twelve thirty when Mom and Ben got back. Peter and I swore to them that we'd clean the whole house the next day and sent them to bed.

"That was one fine party," I said, debating whether to tell him about Andy and deciding not to. I could tell him later in the week.

"It was good," Peter said. "Of course I'm not sure I'll be able to make it back to the bedroom."

"Are you okay?" I asked nervously. "Do you need your wheelchair?"

"I'm fine," he said, laughing. "Exhausted, that's all. I haven't done that much socializing in years."

"You scared me," I said.

"I'm sorry," he said.

He looked so cute sprawled out in the easy chair. I walked over to him and planted an enormous kiss on his forehead.

"I love you, Peter," I said. "Now get to bed. We have a lot of cleaning to do tomorrow."

"Help me?" he said.

So I helped him get up and we walked to his bedroom together.

We stood there for a moment and I became very aware that he was about to kiss me. I didn't want him to, didn't want to have to cope with the after-math of what would have been a purely post-party-euphoria kiss, so I ducked out from under him. "Go to bed," I called. "I'll turn out the lights."

"Yeah," Peter said and opened his bedroom door. "Turn out the lights, Leigh, why don't you."

"Peter," I said, but it was too late. He'd already closed the door. I thought about going in but decided against it. Let Peter be silly if he wanted. Andy had finally asked me out, and I wasn't going to let anyone spoil my mood.

Granted, I hadn't had many dates, but this one was still the worst date of my life.

It wasn't as though I hadn't looked forward to it enough. I'd thought about little else all week. I had debated with Mom three times about what I should wear before finally going out and buying a new outfit. I wanted to look perfect.

Andy picked me up right on time. He was wearing jeans. I wasn't expecting a tuxedo, but I felt overdressed in comparison. He came in briefly, said hello to Mom, Ben, and Peter, and then we walked over to the movie theater, where, except for the sharing of a box of popcorn, we ignored each other for two hours.

Maybe it was the movie's fault. It was a very depressing movie with a lot of people suffering and dying, and even more people drinking. Every time somebody drank liquor, I flinched, which Andy must have noticed, since he had his arm around me. I must have felt like a jackrabbit to him.

"That certainly was an interesting movie," Andy said when the lights went on and we were released.

"Yes," I said. "It certainly was interesting."

"Would you like to go someplace now?" he asked. "We might run into some kids at Juniors."

Juniors was the local hangout. We had one just like it on *The Kampbell Kids*, so I always felt at home there.

"Sure," I said, so we walked over to Juniors. Sure enough, Cathy and Dan and Bob and Sharon were there. Soon I was talking to Cathy, and Andy and Dan were playing pinball. Bob and Sharon danced.

"How's it going?" Cathy asked me.

"Fine," I said. "Only I've talked more with you than I have with Andy."

As though he'd heard me, Andy came back to our booth. "I think maybe we'd better be going," he said. "Come on, Leigh."

"All right," I said and put on my coat. Andy tried to help me, but he just got the sleeves tangled. "I'll see you Monday," I said to Cathy. She nodded, and we said good-bye to the others and left. We walked home in almost complete silence. This was certainly not the date I'd dreamed about all year long. I thought we'd dance and laugh and kiss softly in the moonlight.

"Well," I said when we reached my front door.

"Well," Andy said.

"Thank you," I said. "I had a very nice time."

"You did?" Andy said. "I mean, I'm glad."

"I had a terrible time," I said. "How about you?"

"Rotten," he said.

"Maybe it was the movie," I suggested.

"No," he said. "It was us."

"Oh," I said. "Can't we blame it on the movie?"

"It's dumb," he said. "I've known you for months now but as soon as I'm in a social situation with you, I tense up."

"It's not your fault," I said. "You're not the only one with preconceptions."

"What do you mean?" he asked.

"For a long time I wanted to go out with you, not because I liked you, but because I liked who you were," I said. "Class president, real popular. You were my dream image of the perfect date."

"Really?" Andy said.

"Don't smile," I said. "I didn't mean it as a compliment."

"I'm sorry," he said. "It just sounded like one."

"What I'm trying to say is that I had this image and it had nothing to do with reality," I said. "This was supposed to be the kind of date Chris Kampbell used to go on. Only she didn't go to depressing movies, and her dates never dumped her to play pinball with their best friends."

"I'm sorry about that," he said.

"I'm sorry too," I said. "I always forget it's easier with a script."

"This was the worst date I've ever been on in my life too," he said. "What are you doing tomorrow night?"

"Nothing," I said.

"Good," he said. "Only no movies and no Juniors. Just you and me. We'll go for a walk. If you don't mind the cold."

"I don't mind," I said. "I'd like that."

"Fine," he said. "I'll pick you up at eight."

"I'll see you then," I said.

We looked at each other for a moment, and then he turned away. I let myself in. Peter was alone in the living room.

"Where is everybody?" I asked.

"I convinced them to go to the movies," Peter said. "How was your date?"

"It was awful," I said.

"Really?" he said. "How so?"

"Take my word for it," I said. "But we're giving it another try tomorrow."

"Quitters never win?" he said.

"Something like that," I said. "Look, Peter, I really don't feel like talking about it."

"Okay," he said. "Want to watch TV?"

"I don't think so," I said and went to my room. I sat on my bed for a long time, thinking about Andy and boys and life in general. But mostly I hoped my next date would be a little more romantic.

On Saturday night, I put on jeans and a shirt and was very pleased when Andy showed up dressed almost identically. He exchanged small talk with everybody and then we went out. We just started walking and talked about everything. We discussed school and our friends and what we dreamed about. Andy was going to go to college and then join the Peace Corps before going to med school. I told him that I envied him his ambitions. I had none, I said. I had no idea of what I should do with my life. All my life I'd had plans for what to do, and now, except for school, I had none.

"You'll know what to do when the time comes," he said.

I wasn't so sure, but it was comforting to have

him say it. We walked, holding hands, for well over an hour, in spite of the temperature. Then we turned around and walked to Juniors. This time, though, we didn't join anybody. We found a booth all our own and killed over three hours sitting there drinking sodas and sharing plates of french fries so we wouldn't get kicked out. When anybody came over to join us, we made it obvious we wanted to be alone, and except for a little teasing, our wishes were respected.

I got home after midnight. Andy kissed me good-night outside. In his own way he kissed every bit as well as Barry. I would have invited him in, but I could see the TV set was on, and that meant somebody was up and I didn't feel like sharing Andy just then.

"I'll see you Monday," he said.

I nodded.

"And Tuesday and Wednesday and Thursday and Friday and then Friday night and Saturday night too," he said. "All right?"

"Perfect," I said.

"You're so beautiful," he said. "So beautiful and so special."

We kissed again.

"I'm glad we finally found each other," he said. "It was worth waiting for."

"It was, wasn't it," I said, and we kissed a last good-night. "Take care," I told him. "Walk carefully."

"You're crazy," he called back to me, but he said it fondly. I walked into the house. Peter was sitting in the living room all alone.

"Angie and Ben are in bed," he said. "I thought I'd stay up and say hello."

"Hello," I said dreamily.

"How did it go?" he asked.

"It was fantastic," I said. "It was the best evening of my life. It was just wonderful."

"Oh," he said. "I gather you had a good time."

"Peter, Andy is so wonderful," I said. "He wants to do such good things with his life, and he's so funny too. At Juniors, you know what he did?"

"Look, Leigh, I'm really kind of tired," Peter said. "Can the stories wait?"

"Sure," I said. "You feel okay?"

"I feel fine," he said. "Honestly, a person can't even be tired in this house without it being a major medical emergency."

"I was just asking," I said.

"You asked and I answered," he said. "Goodnight, Leigh. I'll see you in the morning."

"Sure," I said. "Sleep well." I giggled.

"What's so funny?"

"It's just that I told Andy to walk carefully," I said.

Peter stared at me.

"You had to be there," I said.

"I think I'm glad I wasn't," he said and went to his room.

I watched TV for a few minutes, until I was relaxed enough to go to bed. But even then it took me a long time to fall asleep. I kept thinking about Andy instead.

Chapter
11

Andy wasn't the only one concerned about my future plans. My guidance counselor called me in to discuss the exact same topic.

"You ought to be thinking about the future, Leigh," she said to me. "Tell me, what are your future plans?"

It was embarrassing to tell her the truth, which was that I had none, but I had no other choice. I left her office after being showered with names of books I should read and colleges I should consider. I didn't even know if I wanted to go to college.

I supposed I did. I'd always planned to, but never just college. Always work and college. And did I really want to go to college without working at the same time? True, I was enjoying not acting, but I wasn't sure I wanted six straight years of it. But maybe I did. Maybe I should be a premed major like Andy and devote myself to noble works. Like curing hemophilia. Or maybe I should major in theater and learn how to direct. I had really enjoyed helping Anna, Cathy, and Andy with their parts. Maybe I shouldn't major in anything, and just go to a college with continual parties. Or maybe I shouldn't go to college at all, and just get a job at a five-and-ten, and then years from now somebody would do a *Whatever Became of* book and they'd find me behind the candy counter at Woolworth's.

"What are your future plans?" I asked Peter.

"What?" he asked me. The question had come out of nowhere; we'd been discussing whether I should try out for cheerleader next year.

"Your future plans," I said. "Andy has wonderful future plans and I was wondering if you did too."

"I'd hate to compare my future plans with Andy's," Peter said. "I doubt I could compete in such holy waters."

"Maybe you don't have future plans?" I asked hopefully.

"Sure I do," he said. "They're just a little more mundane than Andy's."

"Like what?"

"Barring setbacks in my health, I'd like to go to college . . ."

"Have you decided which one yet?" I asked. Peter had applied to two colleges, one in New York and another in North Carolina. Ben wasn't against the idea of Peter's taking a year off before starting school, but Peter was determined to start in September and take his chances. He'd only grown one inch all year, and his health had been pretty good.

"Whichever one accepts me," Peter said.

"Oh, Peter," I said. "They'll both accept you." No college would dare turn him down, in my opinion. I wasn't sure which one I thought he ought to go to. On the one hand, New York was nice and convenient and it meant I could continue to see a lot of him. On the other hand, Peter would have a better chance at an independent life in North Carolina, and that would probably be better for him, Mom, and Ben. So I wasn't sure.

"Okay," he said. "I'll go to college and I'll major in history."

"History?" I said. "Why history?"

"You sound disappointed," he said. "I told you I'm not as noble as Andy."

"It's not that," I said. "It's just history is so dull."

"Not to me," he said. "I really like it. I'd like to teach it on the college level and do some research. Or maybe just write history. Latin American history fascinates me."

"I didn't know that," I said.

"I don't tell you everything," he said.

"You don't?" I said.

"No," he said, looking amused. "Some things I do keep to myself. The less than fascinating stuff."

"I tell you everything," I said.

"No you don't," he said.

"Everything that counts," I said.

"I guess I'm a secretive person," Peter said. "It comes from years of not having anybody to confide in."

"But you have me now," I said.

"For the time being," he said.

"Forever," I said.

"Yeah, maybe," he said. "Anyway, you know about my future plans. What are yours?"

"I don't know," I said. "I know for the immediate future. Will that do?"

"It depends what they are," he said.

"I'm going to keep dating Andy," I said.

Peter laughed. "I don't think that's the basis for the rest of your life," he said. "Unless you're planning to marry Andy next year."

"Oh no, of course not," I said. "Peter, is it normal not to know?"

"Of course," he said.

"But you're going to be a historian and Andy's going to be a doctor and Cathy's going to be a geologist—a geologist, can you imagine—and Anna isn't sure what she's going to be, except it's going to be something artsy, and I don't even know if I want to go to college."

"Do you want to go back to acting?"

"No," I said.

"Never?" he asked.

"I don't know," I wailed. "If I knew that, don't you think I'd know my future plans? I just don't know. And I feel so weird."

"Don't feel weird," Peter said. "Not knowing what you want to do is perfectly normal. Nowhere is it written that a sixteen-year-old should have made all the major decisions in her life."

"But you know," I said.

"I've spent a lot of my life lying in bed thinking about my future," Peter said. "And I've been able to eliminate a lot more possibilities than most people just because those options aren't realistic. That doesn't mean you should."

"So it's normal for me not to know just yet," I said.

"As normal as apple pie," he said. "Don't worry, Leigh. You are one normal American teen-ager."

But there were occasional reminders that I wasn't all that normal. One came when I was sick with a cold and stayed home from school. Having established to my own and Mom's satisfaction that I was much too sick to be expected to do school work, and not having Peter to talk to since he and Jim were busy, I turned on the TV to watch the soap operas.

I was half-asleep by the time *Joys and Sorrows* came on, but I woke up immediately as soon as I saw what was going on. Because they started the show with a giant close-up of my father's dead face.

Now I've been around for a while and I know the difference between make-believe and real life, but I admit for one moment my heart stopped beating. And then the camera pulled away to a long shot and I saw one of those characters I didn't know very well standing over the remains of what had been Lefty O'Roarke, brandishing a gun about. And then the cops burst into the room and whoever was holding the gun said, "I didn't do it. I didn't do it. But that Lefty O'Roarke had it coming to him. He's dead and I'm glad."

Poor slob, I thought idly. She's due for a long murder trial. And then the enormity of what I was watching hit me. If Lefty O'Roarke had met his just deserts, my poor father was out of work. Soaps rarely keep corpses on their payroll.

As soon as the show ended I called Dad. They taped two weeks ahead so the odds were he was already unemployed. Sure enough, he answered the phone.

"I just saw," I told him. "Dad, I'm so sorry."

"Don't cry about it, honey," he said. "It's just a job."

"I'm not crying," I said. "I have a cold."

"I've heard that one before," he said.

"Do you know who killed you at least?" I asked.

"I know," he said. "We taped the murder to use as flashbacks. But I'm not allowed to tell anybody. Not even you."

"It wasn't Lynn, was it?" I asked.

Dad laughed. "No, Lynn has a perfectly good alibi," he said.

"That's good," I said. "Dad, what are you going to do?"

"Look for a job," he said. "I've been out of work before."

"Are you going to stay in New York or go back to the coast?" I asked. "Or don't you know yet?"

"I'm going to stay in the city for a while," he said. "See if something comes up. Another soap maybe, or a Broadway show. And it's getting to be

169 ⌒

summer stock season. Worst comes to worst, I can do dinner theaters or tour with something."

"But you don't have any offers yet?" I asked.

"Honey, I've only been out of work for a couple of weeks," he said. "And I'm not exactly Robert Redford. My agent is checking out a couple of things. If they fall through, something else'll come up. I have plenty of money saved up from the show, so I'm not about to go bankrupt."

"If you need money, you can borrow it from me," I said.

"That's very sweet of you," Dad said. "But I've never borrowed money from you in the past and I'm not about to start now. Besides, I don't think the need is going to arise."

"Keep me posted," I said. "I worry about you."

"Of course I'll tell you," he said. "Now get over that cold and get back to school. And don't worry."

"All right," I said, and we hung up. Of course I'd worry. At the lowest part of Dad's career he was out of work for close to two years. Fortunately I was working steadily then and we were able to live off my salary, so Dad didn't have to get a job as a shoe salesman or anything like that while he waited for his break. Now he had Lynn to help him until his next job. I only wished he were more the leading man type. Hoods had such hard times keeping jobs.

Still, as Mom pointed out immediately, that was Dad's problem and as an actor he ought to be used to it. Steady work was the exception. Dad was actually pretty lucky to have worked as regularly as he had. Peter was a bit more sympathetic.

"I know how it is," he said. "You want your parents to be settled down, comfortable."

"There's nothing worse than being an unemployed actor," I said. "It can really drive you crazy."

"Can it?" Peter asked, looking funny.

"I mean involuntarily unemployed," I said hastily. "Not retired like me."

"I hope your father gets a job soon," Peter said. "If being out of work is really a fate worse than death."

"It's bad enough," I said. "But colds are worse. I'm supposed to have a date with Andy Saturday night, but I'm not sure I'm going to live that long. I hate being sick."

"It's the weather," Peter said. "The way it's turning into spring."

"Is that what it's doing?" I asked. "I thought it was just turning into slush."

"Slush is the first sure sign of spring," Peter said. "Followed by pollen counts and sinus headaches."

"It sounds wonderful," I said. "Tell me more."

"After spring comes summer," Peter said. "Summer's the time when your legs are in casts. So they can sweat more."

"I remember from last summer," I said. "I felt so sorry for you."

"Never again," Peter said. "I'm going to be disgustingly healthy for the rest of my life."

"Is that a promise?" I asked.

"It's a promise," Peter said. "Unless you give me that cold."

"That's what I'm here for," I said, aiming my next sneeze at him. "How dare you be healthy when I'm on my deathbed?"

"It's the law of compensation," Peter said. "Or God rewarding the virtuous. I forget which."

I threw a half dozen used tissues at him. "You drive me crazy," I said fondly as he picked up the tissues and threw them into the wastepaper basket.

"That's okay," Peter said. "Because I think I would have gone crazy without you."

"And this is the way you reward me?" I asked. Inwardly, though, I was very pleased. I knew I'd been good for Peter, but it was nice having him say it.

"You've been rewarded enough," he said. "You got what you wanted. Friends, a boyfriend, a normal life."

"Thanks to you," I said. "And all your poking and prodding and bossing me around."

Peter grinned. "We did a good job," he said.

"We overcame great obstacles," I said. "Braids and made-for-TV movies and Mr. Taylor."

"Yeah," Peter said. "We've had our share of obstacles."

I thought for a second about how petty my problems were compared to his. "We're a great team," I said. "Together we could conquer the world."

"I know," Peter said. "With my looks and your brains, there's nothing we can't do."

"You are good-looking," I said, examining him carefully. "All my friends think so."

"You talk about me with them?" he asked.

"You are a main topic of conversation," I said. "And the consensus is you're cute. Cathy thinks so in particular."

"Cathy's a nice girl," Peter said. "Besides having excellent taste."

"Why don't you ask her out?" I said. I wouldn't mind Peter dating now that I had Andy.

"No," Peter said.

"But, Peter," I said.

"I don't want to ask her out," Peter said.

"She'd say yes if you asked," I said.

"I'm not going to ask," he said. "End of subject."

"But—"

"No," he said firmly.

"But why not?"

"Look," he said. "We've been honest with each other, right?"

I nodded.

"We've also been honest when there's been something we don't want to talk about. When you were depressed I respected your wishes not to talk about it, didn't I?"

"You were very good about it," I said.

"If we didn't respect each other's privacy, we'd have gone crazy a long time ago," Peter said. "I don't force you to confide, you don't force me."

"It never occurred to me there was some deep dark secret involved," I said. "I just wondered why you wouldn't ask a perfectly nice girl for a date when she's dying to be asked. That's all."

"You're right," Peter said. "That's all. End of discussion."

"If you're sensitive about your limp, you shouldn't be," I said.

"Leigh!" Peter shouted.

"I'm sorry," I said. "I won't mention it again."

"Thank you," he said, getting up. "Now if you'll excuse me."

"I didn't mean to chase you out," I said.

"You didn't chase me," he said. "I'm tired, that's all."

The last thing I wanted was for Peter to be

angry at me. "I'm really sorry," I said. "You're right, we do have to respect each other's privacy. I'm sorry I overstepped the boundaries."

"You're forgiven," Peter said and smiled. "I'm sorry I shouted."

"You should be," I said. "You scared me."

"With your looks and my temper," he said. "Who knows. We could conquer Nebraska."

The next day my cold was better and I went to school. At lunch I made a point of getting Cathy alone and telling her that I didn't think she should hope too much that Peter would ask her out.

"I can guess why," she said.

"Yeah?" I said, knowing I shouldn't ask. "Why?"

"Oh, Leigh," Cathy said. "Can't you tell?"

"Tell what?" I asked.

Cathy shook her head. "Honestly," she said. "I know you've lived in a kind of a cocoon, but sometimes you just amaze me."

"It's his health, isn't it," I said. "I told him not to be self-conscious about his limp, but I think he is. And he's shy too, because of his health. He just hasn't had that much chance to socialize, so he's nervous about it."

"He isn't nervous around you," Cathy said.

"That's different," I said. "I'm there all the time. We had to learn to get along real fast or else it would have been awful on all of us."

"I'm sure his health is a factor," Cathy said.

"You don't think that's all of it?" I asked.

"I could be wrong," she said. "I've been wrong about things often enough in my life."

I could see she didn't think she was wrong. "Come on, Cathy," I said. "What do you think? I know Peter likes you, so that can't be it."

"Leigh, if I'm right you'll find out sooner or later," she said. "And if I'm wrong a lot of people could be embarrassed, myself included. So I think I'll keep my theories to myself for a while. All right?"

"All right," I said, since I obviously had no choice.

Chapter 12

Peter might have his secrets, and Cathy hers, but I didn't have any those lovely spring days. I talked about Andy to everybody, except Peter, who'd made it obvious even to me that he wasn't interested in the subject. And with Andy I talked about all the rest of my life, except for Peter. Andy seemed to be jealous of Peter, although I kept telling him there was no reason to be.

So we talked about upcoming tests and papers and what we would be doing our senior year and what colleges we might go to and what we'd do after college. Andy talked considerably more about his plans than I did, since I still didn't have any idea.

"It all seems so far away," I said.

"It really isn't," he said. "It's never too early to plan for your future." He always looked so cute when he said things like that.

"I suppose," I said, but I didn't believe it. I was enjoying spontaneity and watching the daffodils bloom too much just then to worry about what I would be doing in five years' time. Or three, or even one. The secret to life, I decided that spring, was letting it take care of itself.

I had finally worded my brand-new philosophy of life to my satisfaction as I walked home from school one day. Andy had track practice, so I was alone while I walked. It gave me more of an opportunity to philosophize.

Mom was waiting for me in the living room when I got home. She looked tense. So I put my philosophy away along with my jacket and asked her what the matter was.

"Nothing," she said. "You got a call from your father."

"What did he want?" I asked.

"You'll have to ask him," she said. "I told him you'd call back."

"Okay," I said. "Where's Peter?"

"At therapy," she said. "I should be going to pick him up soon."

I went to the kitchen and dialed Dad's number. He answered on the second ring.

"Hi, Dad," I said. "Mom said you called. What's up?"

"I am," he said. "I have some great news for both of us."

"You're marrying Lynn," I said. "Dad, that's great."

"That's not it," Dad said. "Although Lynn told me to say hi to you."

"Hi back," I said. "So what is it, Dad?"

"I've been offered a job," he said. "A four-month tour of *The Diary of Anne Frank*."

"That's great," I said. "Where will you be touring?"

"All over the country," Dad said. "As a matter of fact, there's even talk if it goes over really well of bringing it to New York for a limited run. You know, a revival."

"Dad, that's just fantastic," I said. "Who do you play?"

"That's just it," Dad said. "I play Anne's father. The director says he sees paternal qualities in me. Can you believe that? But there is one condition."

"What's that?"

"They want me to supply my own teen-age daughter for the part," he said.

"You get to cast the role?" I said. "Gee, Dad, there are a lot of good teen-age actresses around."

"They want you, silly," Dad said. "What do you say?"

"Wait a second," I said. "Are you offering me a job?"

"Indirectly," Dad said. "The producers want the two of us."

"Do you really want to leave New York for that long?" I asked. "What about Lynn?"

"They may cast her as my wife," Dad said. "She's been thinking about leaving *Joys* for a while now."

"That's certainly intimate," I said, my mind reeling.

"Come on," Dad said. "Say that you'll do it. The two of us working together. It would be just like old times."

Old times consisted of one *Kampbell Kids* episode that I'd wrangled a part for Dad on.

"It's a first-class production," Dad said. "We'll be touring all the better summer theaters. Good hotels. It'll be more like a vacation than anything else, traveling all over the country. Plenty of time for being a tourist."

"Dad, I don't know," I said. "Is this the only thing you have lined up?"

"Yeah," Dad said. "But you know I wouldn't push you into anything just for my sake. I've weathered periods of unemployment before; I can manage another one."

Hurt pride. Just what I needed. "I know, Dad," I said. "I was just asking."

"These people love your work," Dad said. "And they love the idea of a father and daughter working together, playing a father and daughter. It's a natural for publicity."

"Yeah," I said.

"Good terms," he said. "You know I wouldn't involve you in any second-rate thing. And you know, honey, it's not good for an actor to be out of work too long. Out of the public eye. They forget you so easily."

I wasn't sure whether he was talking about himself or me. "Dad, I'm really going to have to think about it," I said. "When do they have to know?"

"By Friday," Dad said. "Rehearsals start in April, and we tour from May fifteenth through September."

"But I have school then," I said.

"Arrangements can be made," Dad said. "You should know that."

"Yeah, I know," I said. "Look, Dad, give me a couple of days, and I'll think about it."

"Okay," Dad said. "But if you have any questions, don't hesitate to call me and ask. Did I tell you about the pay?"

"No," I said.

"Good money," Dad said. "Not great, but good. And a percentage of the net for you."

"My very own percentage of the net," I said. "I'm a star."

"You are, honey," Dad said. "That's just how you'd be treated. None of this second-rate after-Barry Cooper business. This would be Leigh Thorpe all the way. And her father coming along for the ride."

And her father's girl friend, I thought, but didn't say so. Instead I told him again I'd think about it and we hung up. I walked back to the living room. Mom was standing by the hall closet, getting out her jacket.

"Hoo boy," I said. "Do you know?"

"I know," she said. "Your father told me all about it this afternoon."

"What do you think?" I asked.

"The terms sound good," she said. "And I know one of the producers; he's a good man. You won't be treated shoddily."

"So you think I should take it?" I asked.

"I didn't say that," Mom said.

"You think I shouldn't," I said.

"I think it's your decision and you'll have to decide for yourself," Mom said. "I have to pick Peter up now."

"Mom, you're not helping at all," I said.

"I'm sorry," she said. "I'll talk to you about it if you want. But I can't decide for you." She put on her jacket, and left.

Every instinct I had told me not to take the job. I'd spent months trying to reach some level of normalcy and I finally had. I was one of the crowd. I had a boyfriend I really liked. I was doing well in school and except for a nagging uncertainty about what I'd be doing with the rest of my life, my problems were down to a bare minimum. I liked my life, loved it actually, and doing this show, no matter how first-class it might be, would ruin it all.

But there was Dad to consider. Who knew when he'd get another decent offer? And something in his voice made me sure we were a package deal. If they didn't get both of us, they just might not use him. If I turned it down, what kind of daughter did that make me?

It was a good part too, one I could handle, but

it would be a challenge. There aren't that many really good roles for teen-agers, as good as Anne Frank.

And I'd be the star. Even if it was just of a summer stock touring company. I'd be the star. Name above the title. People coming out to see me. Me getting the curtain calls, the bouquets of flowers.

Damn. It seemed grossly unfair that my life should have so many complications in it.

There was no one I could consult either. Cathy wouldn't understand the implications. Anna wouldn't understand the hesitation. And Andy wouldn't understand my even considering it. That left just my agent, my guidance counselor, and Peter.

My agent would give me the same sort of advice Mom would; she'd look at it from a purely business point of view. My guidance counselor wouldn't know what the hell to tell me. And Peter would kill me.

The only solution was to go to my bedroom, get into bed, and hope I'd wake up and discover it was all a dream. So I went in, hopped into bed, and stayed wide awake, trying to sort out my thoughts.

Ben! He was a sensible person, except when it

came to Peter. He'd be able to tell me what to do. I checked my watch and found it was still early enough to call him at work. So I looked up his number and called.

"Hi, Ben," I said after I'd been put through. "I was wondering if you could help me with a little problem I have."

"Your father's offer," Ben said. "I know all about it. Your mother called me this afternoon."

"Good," I said. "What should I do?"

Ben laughed. "I think you should make a list of all the pros and cons and make up your own mind," he said.

"Come on, Ben," I said. "What's your advice?"

"That is my advice," he said. "Leigh, I'm totally unequipped to advise you from a business point of view. I don't know if it's a good offer."

"Mom says it is," I said. "Do you think that should be what decides me?"

"That should be a factor, obviously," Ben said. "But there are a lot of other factors and you're going to have to consider each and every one of them very carefully."

"Whatever happened to interfering parents?" I asked.

"They're still around," Ben said. "But I'm not one of them, at least not in this matter. I'd be delighted to talk to you about it, but I certainly won't decide for you."

"I wish somebody would," I said. "Ben, it's my father."

"I know," he said.

"But it's my life too," I said. "And acting is part of my life also. I've always acted. I'm probably crazy to be giving it up before I'm seventeen."

"Uhm," Ben said.

"But I like not working," I said. "I like my life just the way it is and if I take this job it'll never go back to being the way it is now. It's not fair."

"Maybe not," Ben said. "But you should be glad the problem is that you have a choice to make. A lot of people never have any choices at all."

"That's small comfort," I said. "But thanks for trying."

"We'll talk about it after supper," he said. "We'll make those lists."

"Peter's going to hate it if I take the part," I said.

"Don't let Peter make up your mind for you," Ben said sharply. "It's your decision, not his."

"I know," I said. "Thanks, Ben. I'll talk to you later."

We hung up. I put the pillow over my head and wondered if suffocation was the answer.

Dinner was, to put it mildly, tense that night. Mom had obviously included Peter in her briefings because as soon as he came in he said, "Don't do it," to me.

"Peter!" Mom said sharply.

"I don't care," Peter said. "You guys can be neutral. I'm not. I think it would be crazy for Leigh to do it, and I refuse to make a secret of it."

"It's okay, Mom," I said. "I know I'm the one who's going to have to decide."

"What's to decide?" Peter asked. "You can't possibly give up everything you have here."

"I'm thinking about it," I said. "It's complicated, okay? Give me some time and I'll let you know."

"Good," Mom said. "Whatever you decide will be fine with us. Peter included."

"Thanks, Angie," Peter said. "You'd be crazy," he muttered to me.

I thought about discussing it after dinner, the way Ben had suggested, but there didn't seem much to discuss. Mom and Ben had obviously taken vows of neutrality, and Peter equally obviously hadn't. I wasn't going to get a decent objective opinion out of any of them, and even if I could, it wouldn't answer my questions. No matter how objective Mom could be, she couldn't compute in factors like loyalty to my father and the yearning for curtain calls. Or, on the other side, dating Andy and not having to make special arrangements to take my finals on the road.

But I had to talk to someone. Someone who liked me and knew the business and could be objective.

So I called Barry. I got right through to him and told him my story. "So what should I do?" I asked him.

"Take the job," Barry said.

"What?" I said.

"I said take it," he said. "You wanted my advice, didn't you?"

"Yeah," I said. "I was just surprised you gave it to me."

"If you take the job you'll work for a few months and then you'll come back to your home and your school and things won't be exactly the same, but they won't be all that different," he said. "If you don't take it you'll always wonder if you should have. And an actor should act. I know. I've been going crazy."

"When do you start rehearsals?" I asked.

"August," he said. "And it scares me, how little work I've done this year. You've been acting since you were born. It's what you do, it's what you are. You know you've missed it. Here's a chance to get back in to it. Grab it."

"Thank you," I said, feeling a little breathless. "Do you think I'd be crazy if I didn't?"

"No," Barry said. "Obviously, it's your decision,

and you can decide better than me. But if it were me, I'd take the job."

I hung up and I made a list, writing down all the pros and cons. I stared at it every morning when I woke up and every night when I went to bed. I ignored Peter, who kept muttering "You'd be crazy" at me every time Mom or Ben wasn't around. I held hands with Andy during lunch, but I couldn't bring myself to talk to him or any of my friends about it. I wondered why I couldn't. Friends were supposed to understand problems like that. And I realized that much as I loved them, I was different, and there were things they just couldn't understand. None of them had ever worked for a living.

By Wednesday night I knew what I was going to do, but I gave myself until Thursday in case I decided to change my mind. Thursday I felt the same way I had Wednesday, so when I got home from school, I called Dad.

"You've got yourself a costar," I said.

"That's fantastic," Dad said. "I knew it was too good an offer for you to turn down. I'll call the producers immediately and I'll let you know when they'll want us to get together."

"Great," I said, trying to sound like I meant it. "And, Dad, I really look forward to us working together."

"I do too," he said. "A whole summer together. It'll be marvelous for both of us."

Who knew? It might even be. I got off the phone and went into the living room to tell Mom and Peter my decision.

"Fine," Mom said. "I think in your place I would have made the same decision."

"Why didn't you say so before?" I asked.

"Because I didn't want to influence you," she said. "It was a hard decision and it had to be yours. But I think you made the sensible choice."

Peter stared at us in horror. "You're crazy, both of you," he said and got up quickly from his chair.

"Peter," I said, reaching out to stop him.

"No," he said angrily, and broke away from me. He wasn't looking where he was going and he walked straight into the edge of the coffee table and bumped his bad knee.

"Are you okay?" I asked as he rubbed it.

"I'm fine," he said and continued to walk to his room.

I looked nervously at Mom. "Don't worry," she said. "Sometimes he walks right into the wall and doesn't even bruise. You can't tell."

"I hope so," I said and got up to go to his room. I knocked on his door but didn't wait for him to invite me in, since I was afraid he wouldn't.

"Are you going to be okay?" I asked. "Does your knee hurt?"

"It's fine," he said. "Would you please leave?"

"I'm leaving," I said. "But I wish you'd listen to reason."

"Go to hell," he said instead, so I left and went to my bedroom, where I cried for a while. When I felt a little better I called Andy.

"You did what?" he said after I'd told him.

"I took a job," I said. "That's all. One measly job."

"One measly four-month job that'll keep you away from here," he said. "I won't see you all summer."

"I'll be back in September," I said. "And I think we may play one of the theaters near here. Westbury maybe, so I should be back for a little bit."

"Great," Andy said. "What am I supposed to do, hang around backstage?"

"You might enjoy it," I said.

"I enjoy my life," he said. "I thought you did too."

"I do," I said. "But I like acting also. Is that so hard to understand?"

"I understand a lot more than you think I do," he said. "I've never been real to you, have I?"

"What do you mean?"

"All this has been a dream for you," he said.

"Just a little fantasy to kill a few months between jobs. All of us, but me especially. I've just been the perfect date for you. Class president. You never cared for me, for who I really am. You just like the image of me, of the two of us together."

"Andy, that's not true," I said, but for the first time I wasn't sure.

"You told me once it was," he said.

"That was before I really got to know you," I said. "I like the Andy I've been dating. The Andy who wants to be a doctor and makes me laugh and worries about his history grades."

"Then how can you decide to leave me so casually?" he asked.

"Oh, Andy," I said. "If you only knew how uncasual a decision it was. But you were the one who said I'd know what to do when the time came. And it did, and I do know."

"You could have talked it over with me," he said. "I bet you talked to Peter about it."

"Peter was on your side," I said. "He isn't speaking to me right now."

"Give him my sympathies," Andy said. "When do you go?"

"Not for a month," I said.

"Still going to Jeff's party with me?" he asked.

"If you want me to," I said.

"Sure," he said. "I'll tell myself I'm Kris Kristofferson in *A Star Is Born*."

"Andy!"

"Only kidding," he said. "Don't get too upset with Peter. Or me either, for that matter. I've just gotten used to the idea of you. It's hard to readjust."

"I know," I said. "Believe me, I know all about readjusting."

I felt a little better after that, although it bothered me that Peter was still in his room. Ben, Mom, and I tried not to notice his absence at supper, and we talked about the plans I'd have to be making.

Talking about going back to work made me feel better. I had missed acting, dammit, and I was looking forward to doing some. It was a good part and it would be fun traveling around, seeing the U.S., and being with Dad, who, if nothing else, was a great tour guide. I was starting to feel excited about the whole prospect when we heard Peter call to his father.

He sounded awful and Ben ran in. "It's his knee," he said, coming out. "I'll give him a transfusion."

"I knew it," I said. "Is it bad?"

"It's very swollen," he said. "Angie, could you make an ice bag?"

193

"Of course," she said and went to the kitchen. I stood by, feeling helpless.

"Is there anything I can do?" I asked.

"I don't think so," Ben said.

Peter started crying in pain then and we all began moving faster. Ben raced into his bedroom and Mom followed him. I stood in the living room, cursing myself.

Mom came out in a minute while Ben stayed with Peter. "I don't like it," she said to me. "I've seen Peter bad before, but this is worse somehow."

"Should you call the doctor?" I asked.

"It's too soon," she said. "The transfusion may stop the bleeding. We'll give it a little time."

The little time dragged into hours. Peter was clearly in agonizing pain in spite of everything Ben and Mom did for him.

"The swelling's getting worse," Mom said as she went to call the doctor.

"Would it help if I went in?" I asked.

"No," she said. "Leave him alone, at least until the doctor sees him."

Dr. Loeb was there within half an hour. He checked Peter over and then he and Ben went into the living room, where they and Mom consulted in whispers. I felt very left out.

"What did he say?" I asked Mom after he left.

Ben had returned to Peter's room, where Peter was still crying.

"He doesn't know," Mom said. "Nobody knows. With luck Peter'll respond to the coagulants and be better soon."

"And without luck?" I asked.

She sighed. "It's too soon to discuss that," she said. "Honey, it's going to be a long night and there's nothing you can do. Why don't you go to bed?"

"I won't sleep," I said.

"You might," she said.

"Okay," I said. "I'll get out of everybody's way. But let me know if there's anything I can do."

"I will," she promised. "Good-night, honey. I'm sorry your decision had to be spoiled this way."

I went to my bedroom and turned on my TV set, using the noise to cover the sound of Peter's groans. When it got pretty late I tried to sleep, but I didn't manage more than a few short naps, and every time I woke up I could hear Peter crying out in pain.

I gave up at six in the morning, dressed, and went into the kitchen. Mom had a pot of coffee brewing, and I took a cup.

"How's Peter?" I asked as Mom joined me.

"No better," she said. "Ben's given him three

195

transfusions, but they haven't seemed to do a thing for him."

"Did he get any sleep?" I asked. "Did you?"

"None of us did," she said. "How about you?"

"A little," I said. "Can't you give him pain-killers?"

"We have," she said. "They haven't helped at all. We're suppose to call Dr. Loeb in an hour. Maybe he'll know what to do."

"I want to see him," I said.

"Honey, I don't think that's a good idea," Mom said. "Not for him or you."

"It can't make him worse," I said. "Please, Mom."

"All right," she said. "But let me ask Ben."

I sipped my coffee until she came back. Ben was with her.

"Peter's very sick," Ben said. "He's half out of his mind with pain."

"I know that," I said. "And I know he's angry at me anyway. But I want to see him, and I think it would be good for him if I did."

"You won't make him more upset?" Ben asked.

"I'll try not to," I said. "Maybe I can calm him down. I helped that other time."

"This is a lot worse," Ben said. "Just be pre-pared."

"I am," I said grimly and took a last gulp of

coffee before going to Peter's room. I didn't knock and it took Peter a moment to realize I was there.

"Get out!" he cried weakly as soon as he saw me.

"I will not," I said. "You cost me a good night's sleep and the least you could do is offer me a chair."

"Forgive me," he said, trying to sound sardonic. "An actress needs her sleep."

"A human needs her sleep," I said, taking the chair next to his bed where he'd have to see me. "Peter, I just want to say I'm sorry, but I have to lead my own life. Even if that means making decisions you don't approve of. Even if it means throwing away everything we've worked for. I just have to."

"You don't understand," he said, his face moist from tears and sweat.

"What don't I understand?" I said. "Explain it to me."

"I love you," Peter said and turned his head away from me.

"Oh," I said and took a deep breath. "Well, this is one fine time to tell me."

"It never came up before," he said and groaned.

"I think I knew," I said. "Everybody's been hinting something of the sort." A lot of things were beginning to be clear to me now.

"How do you feel?" he asked, very softly.

"Oh, Peter, you know I love you," I said.

"Sure," he said.

"Look at me," I said, and Peter turned his head back to face me. "I love you, Peter. You are an integral part of my life."

"Are you busy Saturday night?" he asked with what might have been a smile.

"Already he wants a serious commitment," I said.

"I want to know how you feel," he said, staring straight at me.

It was hard to answer, looking at him in such pain. "I do love you, Peter, but I don't know what kind of love it is."

"You love me like a brother, is that it?" Peter said.

"I don't know," I said. "I've never analyzed my feelings. I know I've been jealous, but I'm not sure why. I just don't know."

"And how will you find out?" he asked, swallowing hard.

I wished I could absorb his pain and free him from it. "Distance," I said firmly.

"So I should be glad you're leaving?" Peter asked. "Are you crazy?"

"I don't expect you to be glad," I said. "I'm not glad. Just be accepting."

"I'm going to get better," he said defiantly. "I'm

going to go to that place in California and do some intensive therapy."

"Good," I said. "I'm sure the tour will include the West Coast. I'll see you then."

He flinched in pain, but when I bent over him he waved me away. "There's more," he said.

"Yes?" I said, not sure what he meant.

"After California," he said, "I'm going to Seattle too. Make peace with my mother. At least give it a try."

"Will Ben let you?"

"He'll let me," Peter said. "I refuse to be an invalid. And I will not be an emotional cripple."

"Oh, Peter," I said.

"Then I'll go to school in North Carolina," he said. "Less ice. More distance."

"Those are beautiful future plans," I said. "Except that I'm going to miss you."

"Good," he said.

"You do understand, don't you," I said. "Why I took the job?"

Peter nodded. "I know," he said. "We gave it a good try."

"The best we could," I said and kissed his forehead. "Get some sleep, okay? I want you to be human when I get back from school."

"You expect a lot," he said, but he closed his eyes. I tiptoed out of his room.

Dr. Loeb came over right before I had to go to school. He checked Peter out and then came into the living room. This time I included myself in the consultation.

"There's a definite improvement," the doctor told us. "Peter's still in a great deal of pain, but the swelling's down and I think the worst of the bleeding is over."

"Thank God," Ben said.

"It's a setback," Dr. Loeb said. "But Peter isn't a quitter. As a matter of fact, he was telling me what his plans were."

"Plans?" Ben asked.

"They're good ones, don't worry," I said. "Look, I have to get to school."

"Are you sure you want to go?" Mom asked. "You can't have slept well last night."

"I'm fine," I said and gave her a quick good-bye kiss. I had a lot of plans to make and explaining to do and good-byes to say. The sooner I began them, the sooner I could start all over again.